Shadows of Echo Park

Adidas Wilson

Published by Financierpro Publishing, 2024.

This is a work of fiction. Similarities to real people, places, or events are entirely coincidental.

SHADOWS OF ECHO PARK

First edition. November 3, 2024.

Copyright © 2024 Adidas Wilson.

ISBN: 979-8227604750

Written by Adidas Wilson.

Table of Contents

Prologue 1
1 3
2 7
3 11
4 16
5 24
6 28
7 32
8 35
9 37
10 41
11 46
12 51
13 56
14 60
15 65
16 71
17 76
18 81
19 86
20 91
21 96
22 101
23 106
24 111
25 116
26 120
27 125
28 130
29 135
30 139
Epilogue 143
Act I: Shadows in the Light 146

Prologue

Echo Park shimmered in the early morning light, its waters a quiet mirror to the Los Angeles skyline. Fog clung to the ground, drifting over the still lake, wrapping the trees and pathways in an eerie calm. The world was silent, caught in the stillness of dawn before the city woke. And yet, for Lily Thompson, it was her last morning in Echo Park, the place she had thought would be her new beginning. She hovered somewhere between presence and absence, feeling the weight of her final hours yet unable to recall exactly how she had ended up here. Her memories of last night were fragmented, like shards of glass in a kaleidoscope, slipping in and out of reach. She saw flashes of neon signs, a stranger's shadow looming, a reflection of her own eyes in the darkness. Then there was a voice—no, footsteps. Someone was walking toward her, their shoes scuffing against the gravel path. Maya Patel had never imagined her first year in Los Angeles would lead her to this moment. She'd come to the city seeking inspiration, armed with nothing but her old camera and a journal of scribbled dreams. But in the weeks since her arrival, she had felt lost, small against the vastness of the city. Restless, she had taken to morning walks around Echo Park, hoping the peaceful silence would soothe her doubts. Today was no different—or so she thought. As she approached the lake's edge, she noticed a dark shape lying on the shore, half-hidden by the fog. Maya's breath caught in her throat. She hesitated, her instinct telling her to turn away, to go home and forget the chill settling in her bones. But something else, something she couldn't explain, compelled her forward. Lily watched as Maya approached, her heart pounding in her lifeless chest. A strange sensation surged within her—a desperate hope that this woman, this stranger, might somehow see her, not just as a body in the morning mist but as a person with a life that had just begun. Maya knelt beside Lily, taking in the sight of the girl's pale face, her delicate features, the single necklace resting against her collarbone. In that moment, she felt an inexplicable connection, as if this girl—this stranger—was trying to reach out, to tell her something. She didn't know her name, her story, or how she had come to be here, but she felt an unshakable resolve take root within her. As the first rays of sunlight touched the lake, illuminating the silent witness that Echo Park had become, Maya whispered softly, "I won't forget you." And at that moment, Lily's spirit seemed to be easy, knowing that someone had finally seen her, that her story might not end here after all.

1

Shadows in the Fog

Maya couldn't sleep that night. Every time she closed her eyes, she saw the girl's face, the hollow look in her eyes, the unnatural stillness of her body. It was as if the girl had followed her home, lingering at the edges of her mind, demanding her to be remembered. She replayed the scene over and over, wondering if there was something she could have done, if only she had arrived sooner. She scrolled through the local news, looking for any mention of the girl by the lake, but there was nothing. No headlines, no photo, not even a vague police statement. It was as if she had vanished into thin air, leaving no trace of her existence behind. Maya pushed herself out of bed, restless. She slipped on her jacket, grabbed her camera, and headed back to Echo Park. She didn't know what she was looking for; maybe some sign, some clue that could tell her more about the girl she'd found. As she wandered the deserted paths, memories of her own arrival in LA flooded back—the lonely nights, the feeling of being lost in a city that didn't care if you made it or not. She felt a strange kinship with this stranger, as if they shared a bond neither of them could explain.

When she reached the spot where she had found the girl, Maya raised her camera, taking a photograph of the lake in the early dawn light. The fog was thick, curling around the trees and the water like ghosts. For some reason, the click of the shutter felt significant, a way of preserving something fleeting, something that had almost disappeared.

Maya moved carefully through the early morning haze, her fingers tight around her camera as she scanned the park. The familiar mist seemed thicker today, clinging to the trees and wrapping themselves around her like a memory she couldn't shake. Every inch of Echo Park felt haunted, as if the shadows themselves held pieces of the girl she'd found.

She snapped a few shots of the lake, its surface calm and dark. The shutter clicks echoed in the quiet, and each image felt like a new piece in a puzzle she had only just begun to understand. She couldn't let go of what she'd seen. The girl's face—the paleness of her skin, the small, delicate necklace, the absence of life in her once-bright eyes—haunted her every thought. Maya had only seen her for a moment, but it felt like that single encounter had carved itself deep into her.

As she stood by the water's edge, she noticed something faint on the ground—a half-erased set of footprints trailing into the fog. Her heartbeat quickened, a thrill of fear and curiosity making her pulse race. She crouched down, snapping a picture, her mind racing. Who had been here, standing in this exact spot? The realization dawned on her: someone else must have been nearby when the girl died. Someone had left these faint marks behind, disappearing into the shadows before dawn broke.

For a moment, Maya hesitated, wondering if she was taking things too far. After all, she didn't know this girl; they had never spoken, never crossed paths before that morning. Yet she couldn't shake the feeling that it was up to her to find out the truth. She felt an unexplainable pull, a feeling that she was supposed to be here, that her own path had crossed with Lily's for a reason.

Later that Day

Back in her tiny, sunlit apartment, Maya sat cross-legged on her bed, staring at her camera's screen. She flicked through the images she'd taken, each one holding a hint of the mystery she was trying to unravel. As she zoomed in on the footprints, she noticed something strange, a faint outline of something small and round next to them, almost obscured by the gravel. A pendant? A button?

She leaned back, chewing on her thumbnail as she considered her next steps. She couldn't stop thinking about the old woman she'd spoken to, the one who had seen the girl at the park. What had she said? That the girl looked lost, like she was waiting for something? Or...someone? Maya's stomach churned at the thought, a mix of excitement and dread brewing within her.

Maya glanced at her laptop, where a blank document stared back at her, the cursor blinking as if urging her to write. Her friends had always encouraged her to blog about her photography, to share the stories behind her pictures. Maybe this was her chance to do something meaningful, to give a voice to someone who had been silenced. She could tell Lily's story—if she could uncover it.

But first, she needed a lead.

The Next Morning

Maya returned to Echo Park just after dawn, following the path around the lake to where she'd seen the girl's body. She half expected the police to be there, finally taking an interest in the case, but the area was deserted, as if nothing had happened. As she walked, she noticed more small clues—a cigarette butt here, a scuff mark on the concrete there. Little details, easy to overlook, but together they felt significant.

She stopped by the bench where the girl had often sat, according to the old woman. As Maya sat down, she looked out at the lake, trying to imagine the view through Lily's eyes. What had she seen here? What had she felt? Loneliness? Hope?

A figure caught her eye—a man standing a little way off, watching her. He wore a worn leather jacket, his face shadowed by the brim of a baseball cap. Maya's breath hitched, and she quickly looked away, pretending to focus on her camera. When she glanced back, he was gone, slipping into the fog as if he'd never been there at all.

Uneasy, she rose from the bench, her heart pounding as she scanned the park. Was he connected to the girl somehow? Or was he simply another lost soul, drawn to Echo Park like so many others?

She didn't know, but she was determined to find out.

Later That Day

After her walk, Maya decided to visit the local police station. She was hesitant, they might think she was overstepping, a meddling stranger trying to play detective. But she felt she had no choice. If no one else was going to investigate this girl's death, then it was up to her to start asking questions.

At the counter, a weary officer looked up at her, barely interested.

"Can I help you?"

Maya cleared her throat, trying to sound confident. "I... I wanted to report something. A... a body I found. In Echo Park, by the lake. It was a few mornings ago."

The officer raised an eyebrow, shifting slightly in his seat. "A body? And you're just reporting this now?"

"I—I tried to forget it," she admitted, flustered. "But I can't. I don't know who she was, but she looked young, like she was new to the city. I just... I can't stop thinking about her."

The officer sighed, scribbling something down. "What did she look like?"

Maya described Lily as best she could, every detail etched into her mind. The officer listened, nodding occasionally, but his face remained unreadable.

"We'll look into it," he said at last, offering a weak smile that didn't reach his eyes. "Thank you for reporting it."

Maya walked out of the station, feeling a mixture of relief and frustration. Part of her knew that the police would treat this as just another tragic statistic, another faceless name in the city's endless sea of cases. But she wasn't going to give up that easily. As she walked back toward Echo Park, the morning sun casting long shadows across the ground, Maya made herself a promise. She would keep searching for Lily's story, no matter how many dead ends she faced, no matter how many strange looks she got. She had seen something that morning, felt a connection that ran deeper than reason. She would find out who Lily was, and she would make sure the city remembered her.

2

Fragments of Life

Lily's memories of her final days in LA were like flashes of a half-finished dream. She could recall her arrival—wide-eyed, excited, filled with that unique kind of hope that only a fresh start could bring. Los Angeles was supposed to be her new beginning, a city where no one knew her, where she could be anyone she wanted to be.

But soon, the glittering dream began to unravel. She had trusted the wrong people, followed the wrong lead, and found herself drawn into the city's shadows. She had fled from something in her past, but here, in LA, she had found herself entangled in new secrets, ones that would cost her more than she ever imagined.

Now, in this ghostly, detached state, she watched Maya with a sense of urgency, an instinctive hope that maybe this stranger would somehow understand the pieces of her story. She couldn't remember much about her last night, but she knew she had been close to something—close to someone. A friend? A stranger? She couldn't remember. All she knew was that her story hadn't ended the way it was supposed to, and Maya was her only hope of making things right.

Lily floated through memories, fragments of her final days surfacing and disappearing like flashes of lightning. The pieces never seemed to form a full picture, leaving her in a fog, much like the one that clung to Echo Park. She tried to recall the details—why she'd come to Los Angeles, the people she'd met, and the tangled web she'd somehow become ensnared in. She remembered bits of laughter, the glow of neon lights, and a shadow that had begun following her as soon as she arrived.

Lily's memories drifted back to her first night in Los Angeles, filled with nervous energy as she explored the city. She remembered her excitement, her belief that here, she could leave everything behind and start fresh. The city lights had felt endless, like a constellation she was only just beginning to understand. But that feeling had been fleeting, lost as quickly as it had come.

And then she remembered the man with the cold eyes, the one who had shown her the city's darker side. She could still see his face in the corners of her mind, though his name remained stubbornly out of reach. He had promised her a shortcut to the dream she was chasing. She had trusted him; thought he was different. But that trust had been her mistake, the first misstep that had set her on the path that ended at Echo Park Lake.

Later That Day

Maya sat at her kitchen table, sipping a cup of coffee as she flipped through the photographs she'd taken at the park. Her gaze lingered on one particular image of the lake; its surface was disrupted only by faint ripples that seemed to reach out like ghostly fingers. It was hauntingly beautiful, and something about it reminded her of Lily's face that morning by the lake, still and silent yet holding a story beneath the surface.

She pulled out the sketchbook she'd found near the girl's body, running her fingers over the worn edges. Inside, there were pages filled with hurried drawings and phrases that seemed almost frantic, scrawled in handwriting that was bold and uneven. The sketches were simple—shapes and symbols she couldn't fully interpret, along with phrases like, "Lost," "Wrong turn," and "No one sees."

But it was the final page that gave her pause. It held a small, intricate drawing of Echo Park, with an arrow pointing to a bench near the lake, the same bench where she had first sat when she returned to the same place. Beneath the drawing were the words, "I am here."

Maya's heart pounded as she stared at the words. Was Lily trying to leave a message? Was she marking the place where she spent her last moments, or was this simply a reflection of her state of mind? Maya didn't know, but she felt a strange, unshakable certainty that this was a clue meant just for her.

She grabbed her camera and headed back to the park, determined to retrace Lily's steps and see if she could uncover more. She found herself at the bench again, sitting down with the sketchbook open on her lap, gazing out at the lake.

At Echo Park

As Maya sat there, her mind racing, she heard someone approach. Turning, she found herself face to face with the same man she'd noticed before—the one in the leather jacket and baseball cap. Up close, his face was sharper, eyes dark and unreadable. He gave her a faint nod, a small smile that didn't quite reach his eyes.

"Nice spot isn't it?" he said, his voice low and smooth.

Maya swallowed, trying to keep her composure. "Yeah, it's... peaceful."

He looked out at the lake, his gaze distant. "You come here often?"

"Not really. I... I just like the view." She didn't want to give away her true reason for being here, sensing that there was something off about this man, something guarded.

He nodded, slipping his hands into his pockets. "You remind me of someone," he said, almost as an afterthought. "A girl who used to come here a lot. Kept to herself. I never got her name."

Maya's heart raced. Was he talking about Lily?

She glanced at him, her curiosity overpowering her caution. "Did you... did you know her well?"

The man shrugged; his gaze still fixed on the water. "Not well. But I'd see her around, always sitting on that bench, scribbling in her notebook. She looked... like she didn't belong here, you know? Like she was out of place."

Maya's pulse quickened. This man had seen Lily, maybe even spoken to her. But there was something about his demeanor that made her wary, as if he knew more than he was letting on.

"Do you know what happened to her?" Maya asked carefully, watching his face for any sign of recognition.

The man's smile faded, his expression hardening. "People like her... they come to the city with big dreams. But LA doesn't care. It chews people up and spits them out." He glanced at her, his eyes cold and unfeeling. "Sometimes they just... disappear."

With that, he turned and walked away, leaving Maya sitting alone on the bench, her heart pounding. She knew she'd have to keep an eye on him. There was something in his eyes, something hidden beneath his calm exterior, that sent a chill down her spine.

That Evening

Back at her apartment, Maya replayed her encounter with the stranger, going over every word, every expression. She could sense that he was connected to Lily somehow, maybe even part of the reason she'd met such a tragic end. But how? And why?

She spent hours scouring the sketchbook, trying to decode the drawings and phrases. The words "No one sees" and "Wrong turn" felt especially ominous, as if Lily had known she was trapped in something dangerous but couldn't find her way out.

Finally, exhausted, Maya set the sketchbook down and turned to her laptop. She started typing, her fingers flying across the keyboard as she documented everything she'd uncovered so far—her encounter with the stranger, the old woman's words, the eerie sketch of Echo Park. It felt cathartic, like she was piecing together a puzzle one clue at a time, even if the full picture was still out of reach.

As she typed, a strange sense of purpose filled her. This wasn't just about finding answers for Lily; it was about finding her own place in the city, her own reason for being here. In some inexplicable way, she felt that Lily's story was now her story too, woven together by the threads of chance and fate.

And as she closed her laptop, she made a vow—to uncover the truth about Lily, no matter how dangerous it might be.

3

The Watcher in the Shadows

Days turned into a blur as Maya struggled to move forward. Her friends urged her to focus on her work, to keep exploring the city, to distract herself from what she'd seen. But every time she tried, her mind drifted back to the girl by the lake.

Her apartment felt smaller than ever, the walls pressing in on her with an almost suffocating intensity. Restless, she spread out the few belongings she'd managed to save from the small sketchbook the girl had left behind, with cryptic drawings and half-finished phrases. They didn't make sense, yet Maya felt that if she could just piece them together, she might unlock some part of the girl's story. As she thumbed through the sketchbook, a single drawing caught her eye: an intricate sketch of Echo Park, drawn from a perspective she couldn't quite recognize. In the corner was a name scrawled in the girl's handwriting— "Lily." For the first time, Maya felt like she was getting closer, like this girl wasn't just a nameless stranger, but someone with a life, a past, a story waiting to be told. The next day, Maya returned to Echo Park, searching for any sign of Lily's presence. She took photographs of the lake, the benches, the trees, hoping to capture something, a shadow, a detail—that might help her understand. She spoke to people who frequented the park, asking if anyone had seen a girl who looked like Lily, describing the necklace, the sketchbook. Most people shook their heads, but one elderly woman paused, her brow furrowing.

"I remember seeing a girl like that," the woman said slowly. "She was here often, always sitting by the water with that little notebook. She seemed... lost, like she was waiting for something."

Maya felt a chill run through her. "Did you ever talk to her?"

The woman shook her head, a hint of regret in her eyes. "No, dear. Sometimes we just watch, you know. We don't think to intervene until it's too late."

As the woman walked away, Maya stood by the water, her hands shaking. She could feel Lily's presence, urging her forward. She wasn't sure why, but she felt certain that finding out more about Lily's last days would bring her closer to something, maybe even a truth about herself that she'd been too afraid to confront. In that moment, standing by the lake, Maya made a silent promise. She wouldn't let Lily's story disappear. She would find out who Lily was, what had brought her to Echo Park, and why she had left this world without a trace.

The following morning, Maya woke up with unfamiliar determination. Despite her fatigue and the eerie encounter with the man in the leather jacket, she knew she couldn't back down now. Lily's story had become something she was compelled to see through, an unshakable thread pulling her deeper into a mystery that felt both dangerous and strangely personal.

She spent her morning searching through the few online resources available, scouring missing persons websites, recent obituaries, and any news articles about young women found dead in Los Angeles. But there was nothing, no mention of a girl fitting Lily's description. It was as though she'd slipped into the city's shadows without anyone noticing, without anyone caring enough to report her missing.

Frustrated, Maya decided to return to Echo Park, hoping to spot another clue she might have overlooked. She packed her camera, notebook, and Lily's sketchbook, then headed out, her mind racing with questions. Was it possible Lily had family somewhere? Friends who were still looking for her? Or had she, like so many people who came to LA, left her life behind, burning every bridge in pursuit of a fresh start?

As Maya walked through the park, she became acutely aware of her surroundings. She kept glancing over her shoulder, half-expecting to see the man in the leather jacket lurking somewhere in the distance. But the park was calm, filled with the usual joggers, dog walkers, and young parents pushing strollers. For the first time since discovering Lily, Maya felt a momentary sense of peace—until she noticed someone watching her from across the lake.

It was a woman, older, maybe in her sixties, with a worn sunhat and a tired look in her eyes. She was staring straight at Maya, her expression guarded, as if she recognized her. Maya felt a chill crawl up her spine. She took a deep breath, walked around the lake, and approached the woman, her steps careful and measured.

"Excuse me," Maya said, forcing a smile. "I couldn't help but notice you looking at me. Do... do we know each other?"

The woman shook her head slowly, her gaze intense. "I saw you here yesterday. And the day before that. You're... looking for her, aren't you?"

Maya's breath caught. "You mean... the girl who was found here?"

The woman nodded, glancing around as if worried someone might overhear. "I used to see her around. Quiet girl, kept to herself. She'd sit by the water, drawing or writing. I never spoke to her, but she looked... troubled."

Maya's pulse quickened. "Do you know anything about her? A name, where she might have been staying?"

The woman hesitated, then shook her head. "No, but... there was something strange. A man was often with her. They never sat together, but I'd see him watching her from a distance, like he was waiting for her to notice him. Sometimes he'd follow her when she left the park. I don't know if she knew he was there."

Maya felt her stomach turn. The description matched the man she'd encountered, the one who had spoken cryptically about people "disappearing." Had he been stalking Lily? Or was there something else, something more sinister, lurking beneath his calm demeanor?

"Do you remember anything else?" Maya asked, desperation edging into her voice. "Anything at all that might help?"

The woman glanced around, looking nervous. "Only that... she seemed to be running from something. Like she was always looking over her shoulder. I think... I think she was scared."

Maya's mind raced with possibilities, each one darker than the last. She thanked the woman and watched her walk away, disappearing into the crowd of parkgoers. Alone once again, Maya felt a chill settle over her. The clues were mounting, but they only seemed to raise more questions. Who was this man, and why had he been watching Lily? And what had she been so afraid of?

That Evening

Back in her apartment, Maya sat on her bed, staring at her laptop screen, the faint glow casting shadows across her room. She had started an anonymous blog, intending to document Lily's story as best she could. She wasn't sure if anyone would read it, but writing it down felt like a way to keep Lily's memory alive, a way to ensure she wouldn't be forgotten.

She typed, recounting everything she knew so far—the girl by the lake, the sketchbook, the mysterious man. She wrote about the older woman's account and her own encounter with him, her fingers moving swiftly over the keys as she wove the story together, piece by piece.

But as she wrote, an uneasy feeling crept into her mind. She glanced at her window, noticing for the first time the shadows outside. For a brief, heart-stopping moment, she thought she saw a figure standing by the tree across the street, looking out her window.

Her breath caught, and she blinked, but when she looked again, the figure was gone. Her imagination was probably playing tricks on her, a side effect of the fear that had been building since the morning she'd found Lily's body. But the feeling of being watched lingered, settling like a weight on her chest.

Maya closed her laptop, locking her doors and windows before heading to bed. But sleep didn't come easily. She tossed and turned, Lily's story replaying in her mind alongside the unsettling gaze of the man at the park. Who was he, and what did he want?

The Next Morning

Maya woke to the sound of her phone buzzing. Groggy, she grabbed it, squinting at the unknown number flashing on the screen. Part of her wanted to ignore it, but a strange sense of urgency compelled her to answer.

"Hello?" she said cautiously.

There was a pause at the other end, then she recognized a low voice.

"You should stop looking into things that don't concern you."

Maya's blood ran cold. It was him. The man from the park.

"How did you get this number?" she demanded, trying to keep her voice steady.

A chuckle, low and menacing, crackled through the line. "You're making things difficult, aren't you? Digging up dirt where it doesn't belong. People like you should learn when to leave well enough alone."

The line went dead, and Maya sat there, her heart racing. Her hands shook as she set her phone down, the reality of the situation settling over her like a dark cloud. She was being threatened, watched—targeted, even. Whoever this man was, he didn't want her finding out the truth about Lily.

But as her fear mingled with anger, Maya realized she couldn't stop now. This man was dangerous, yes, but that only confirmed her suspicions that there was more to Lily's story than a tragic accident.

She would be careful, but she wasn't going to let him scare her away. With renewed resolve, Maya picked up her camera and slipped the sketchbook into her bag. She had a plan forming in her mind, one that would take her closer to the truth about Lily and perhaps bring her face to face with the man who had threatened her.

But this time, she wouldn't be unprepared.

4

Threads of Danger

Maya felt a strange calm as she stepped out of her apartment, the early morning city buzzing softly with life. Her heart still pounded from the phone call, but now there was a sense of focus driving her. She wasn't just digging up pieces of Lily's story anymore; she was unraveling with something darker, something people didn't want to uncover. And that knowledge only strengthened her resolve.

As she reached Echo Park, she took a different route, aiming to observe without being noticed. She wasn't entirely sure where to start, but she had one lead that she hadn't fully explored—the park bench where she'd found the sketchbook. She made her way there, sitting quietly as she glanced around.

The park was quiet this time of day, the early risers filtering in slowly, casting long shadows in the rising sun. Maya tried to stay alert, watching for any sign of the man in the leather jacket, but he was nowhere to be seen. Still, she knew he was close, watching her. His warning call was proof enough.

She took out the sketchbook, turning it over in her hands. Each time she looked at it, new details seemed to jump out—small smudges, faded words, hasty sketches. On a hunch, she held the pages up to the light, tilting them carefully. That's when she saw it: faint pencil marks barely visible on one of the blank pages, as though someone had started to write something, only to stop and erase it.

She ran her fingers over the paper, trying to make out the marks. The words were difficult to decipher, but she could just make out "warehouse" and "third night." Her pulse quickened. She didn't know what it meant, but it was the first tangible clue she'd found—something concrete, something with a place and time.

Without hesitation, she snapped a photo of the faint writing with her phone. Whatever this "warehouse" was, it had to be a significant piece of the puzzle. She could feel it.

That Afternoon

Maya returned home and opened her laptop, searching through maps of the surrounding area. There were several abandoned warehouses near the outskirts of Los Angeles, places that had been shut down and forgotten. She clicked through them, one by one, until her eyes landed on an old shipping depot about a mile from Echo Park. The place had been closed for years, a relic of a time when goods were transported by rail in and out of the city. If there was anywhere Lily might have ended up, this seemed like a plausible lead.

Maya prepared herself, packing a few essentials into her backpack—her camera, flashlight, and pepper spray. She knew she was treading on dangerous ground, especially after the man's warning, but the thrill of getting closer to the truth overrode her fear.

The sun was dipping low in the sky by the time she reached the warehouse district. The area was deserted, with only a few stray cats and pigeons picking through scraps in the alleyways. She walked cautiously, checking over her shoulder now and then. The silence felt heavy, pressing in around her as she approached the warehouse.

At the Warehouse

The building loomed before her, dark and silent. Rusted metal doors hung from their hinges, and broken windows dotted the upper floors. She took a deep breath, steeling herself, and slipped inside, her footsteps echoing against the concrete.

The interior was vast and empty, filled with dusty crates and broken equipment. Shafts of fading sunlight streamed through the broken windows, casting long shadows that danced across the floor. Maya's flashlight beam cut through the darkness, illuminating scraps of paper, discarded bottles, and the remnants of lives that had once passed through these walls.

As she explored, she felt a presence, as though someone or something was lurking just beyond her line of sight. She kept her hand close to her pepper spray, her senses on high alert.

Then, she saw a small, makeshift bed hidden behind a stack of crates. There were blankets, worn and frayed, a few empty food cans, and a crumpled photo pinned to the wall. Maya's heart pounded as she moved closer, shining her flashlight over the photo. It was a faded Polaroid of a young girl who looked almost like Lily, with the same sharp eyes and guarded expression. But there was something different, something older and harder about her. Maya's hands shook as she snapped a picture of the setup, her mind racing. Could this have been where Lily was hiding?

As she continued searching, her flashlight caught on something etched into the floor near the bed symbol, scratched in haste. It looked like a spiral, surrounded by hastily drawn lines and letters. Maya couldn't decipher it, but something about it felt... wrong. She took another photo, wondering if it was a message or a warning.

Suddenly, the sound of footsteps echoed through the warehouse.

Maya froze, her heart pounding as the steps grew closer, slow and deliberate. She turned off her flashlight, crouching down behind a crate, her breath shallow as she listened. The footsteps stopped just a few yards away, and she could make out the shadow of a figure—a man, his silhouette familiar in the fading light.

It was him. The man from the park, the one who had warned her.

Maya's heart raced as she watched him scanning the room, his gaze cold and searching. She held her breath, hoping he wouldn't see her, praying he wouldn't come any closer.

But then he spoke, his voice was low and steady. "I know you're here."

She gripped her pepper spray, ready to defend herself if he got too close. She didn't move, didn't dare breathe, as he took a few more steps, his shadow looming over her hiding spot.

"I warned you," he said, his voice echoing off the empty walls. "Some stories are better left buried."

Maya felt a surge of anger, her fear momentarily overridden. Lily's story wasn't something to be buried; it was something to be told, something to be known. She clenched her fist around the pepper spray, preparing herself to act if he came any closer.

But then, just as quickly as he had arrived, he turned and walked away, his footsteps fading into the distance. Maya stayed hidden, her heart pounding as she listened to the silence settle around her once more.

When she was sure he was gone, she let out a shaky breath, her hands still trembling. She knew now that she was in real danger, but she also knew she was closer to the truth than ever before. Lily's story was unfolding before her, piece by piece, and she was determined to see it through.

That Evening

Back in her apartment, Maya reviewed the photos she'd taken, her mind buzzing with questions. Who was that man, and why was he so determined to keep her from finding out the truth? And what had Lily discovered had driven her to hide in that warehouse?

As she sifted through the photos, she noticed something she hadn't seen before—the scratched symbol near the bed. It was clearer in the photograph, the spiral surrounded by letters that looked like initials. She zoomed in, her pulse quickening as she realized they had spelled out a name: R.G.

Maya didn't know who R.G. was, but she was certain it was another clue, another piece of the puzzle Lily had left behind.

And she knew, with a growing sense of dread, that the man wouldn't be the only danger she'd face in uncovering it.

Maya's apartment felt stifling as she reviewed the photos, the weight of everything she'd discovered pressing down on her. The initials "R.G." etched next to the strange spiral were the only solid lead she had, but they brought with them more questions than answers. She stared at the photograph, willing the letters to reveal something, anything, about who might be behind Lily's death. Who was R.G., and why had Lily felt the need to hide in that dark, empty warehouse?

She searched online, plugging "R.G." into every local missing person, criminal, and business database she could find. Hours passed as she clicked through search results, her mind racing as she sifted through names and faces, hoping for some connection to appear. But nothing matched, and her frustration mounted, mingling with the lingering fear from her encounter with the man in the warehouse. His warning replayed in her mind: Some stories are better left buried.

Determined, she decided to take her search offline. She slipped her notebook and camera into her backpack, along with Lily's sketchbook, and set out to follow a hunch that had been simmering since she'd first met the woman in Echo Park. If the older woman had seen Lily and the man before, maybe someone else in the neighborhood had seen them too. There had to be other people who frequented the park, regulars who might remember a young girl who had seemed lost, or a man who watched her from the shadows.

Later That Evening

The sun was setting when Maya arrived at Echo Park, its light casting a warm glow over the lake. The park was busier than usual, filled with families, joggers, and couples enjoying the fading warmth of the day. Maya made her way to the bench where she'd found Lily's sketchbook, hoping someone nearby might recognize the description of Lily or the man.

She approached a few people, cautiously describing the girl she'd found and the mysterious man in the leather jacket. Most people shrugged, some gave her strange looks, but one woman—a vendor selling hot dogs near the lake—paused as Maya described Lily's appearance.

"Oh, yeah, I've seen her," the vendor said, wiping her hands on a napkin. "Pretty girl, dark hair, always had this look like she was searching for something. She'd sit on that bench for hours, sketching or writing in a little notebook."

Maya's heart raced. "Did you ever see anyone with her? Or anyone watching her?"

The vendor's eyes narrowed, thinking. "There was a guy, sometimes. I'd see him standing by the trees, just watching her. I remember it because it gave me the creeps. Once, I thought about calling out to her, you know, just to see if she was okay. But I didn't. Figured it was none of my business."

Maya thanked the vendor and continued, feeling both exhilarated and unsettled. She was building a clearer picture of Lily's life, her routines, the places she frequented, the people who noticed her. And that strange man seemed to be a fixture in her final days.

As she walked away, she noticed someone watching her from across the path. It was the same man, unmistakable in his worn leather jacket and dark baseball cap, his gaze fixed on her with an unsettling intensity. Maya's heart skipped, but she forced herself to remain calm. She knew he was following her and confronting him alone in the park would be too dangerous.

She turned her back to him and walked calmly toward the exit, every nerve in her body on high alert. As she left the park, she slipped her phone out of her pocket, quickly snapping a photo of him over her shoulder. She didn't know if the image would be clear, but at least she'd have something—a face, a figure, a trace of the man who seemed so intent on keeping her from the truth.

Later That Night

Back in her apartment, Maya reviewed the photo she'd taken, but the image was blurry, the man's face half-obscured by the shadow of his cap. Frustrated, she threw her phone on the bed and sank into her chair, feeling the weight of the day settle over her. She was closer to answers, but every step seemed to pull her deeper into a maze of uncertainty and danger.

She turned to Lily's sketchbook, flipping through it once more. The drawings were haunting, each one more frantic and desperate than the last, as if Lily had been trying to capture some dark truth, she couldn't fully express. At the back of the book, tucked between two pages, Maya found something she hadn't noticed before—a folded piece of paper, so thin it almost seemed to disappear against the pages.

Carefully, she unfolded it, revealing a hand-drawn map of Echo Park and the surrounding streets. Certain areas were marked with small X's, along with a date scribbled next to each one. Maya's pulse quickened as she traced her finger over the marks—these were locations around the park, places Lily must have visited in her final days. And one of the X's was placed directly on the warehouse.

One of the dates was just a few days before Lily's death, marking the warehouse with a faint arrow. It was as if she'd been trying to leave a trail, a map that could be followed if someone was looking close enough.

As Maya examined the map, her phone buzzed with a new message from an unknown number. Her heart pounded as she opened it, dreading pooling in her stomach.

The message was simple: Leave it alone, or you'll be next.

Maya's hands shook, her fear now blending with a simmering anger. Whoever this man was, he thought he could intimidate her into giving up, into walking away from a story that was finally coming to light. But she was done running, done hiding. She was going to find out who R.G. was, no matter the cost.

The Following Morning

Maya spent hours tracing the locations on Lily's map, moving cautiously through the neighborhoods surrounding Echo Park. She photographed each location, looking for any sign of a connection to the initials "R.G." The places marked on the map seemed ordinary at first—an old bookstore, a corner diner, a small hotel on the outskirts of town. But as she studied each one, she noticed a pattern emerging.

At each location, there were faded posters, signs from years ago advertising music nights, poetry readings, and gatherings hosted by a mysterious group called "The Rogue Guardians"—a name that perfectly matched the initials "R.G."

She jotted down the name, wondering if this group was somehow connected to Lily's death. It seemed unlikely that a small community group would pose a threat, but there was something about the worn, faded posters that felt strange, almost foreboding. The Rogue Guardians were nowhere to be found online, no website, no social media presence. It was as if they had disappeared—or gone underground.

With a newfound resolve, Maya made her way to the final location on the map bar tucked into a forgotten corner of downtown LA, barely visible beneath layers of graffiti and grime. The neon sign above the door flickered dimly, casting a ghostly glow over the entrance. She took a deep breath and stepped inside, her senses on high alert.

The bar was nearly empty, with only a few patrons scattered along the counter. She scanned the room, noting a faded Rogue Guardians poster tacked onto the wall, half-covered by torn concert flyers. Her eyes drifted over the people inside, looking for anyone who might recognize Lily or know about her connection with this group.

At the end of the bar sat a man in a dark jacket, his eyes fixed on a drink he hadn't touched. Maya's heart skipped—she recognized him instantly. It was the man from the park, the same one who had warned her, the same one who had followed her through the city's shadows.

Before she could turn away, he looked up, his gaze locking onto hers. A slow, dangerous smile spread across his face, and he beckoned her over, as if he'd been expecting her all along.

Maya's pulse thundered in her ears as she forced herself to approach him, each step heavy with dread. She didn't know what she was walking into, but she knew she couldn't turn back now.

As she reached his table, he gestured to the seat across from him. "I warned you to stop looking," he said, his voice low and smooth. "But I knew you wouldn't listen."

Maya sat down; her hands clenched into fists beneath the table. "I'm not here to listen to your warnings," she replied, her voice steady. "I'm here for answers. Who are you, and why did you follow Lily?"

He chuckled, a dark gleam in his eyes. "Oh, I'm no one important. Just a messenger for people who prefer their secrets kept hidden. And Lily? She was just another girl who thought she could run from her past."

Maya's skin prickled, but she didn't back down. "The Rogue Guardians. Who are they, and what do they have to do with her death?"

He leaned forward, his smile fading. "You're in way over your head, kid. Some secrets are buried for a reason. You dig too deep; you might find yourself right beside her."

Maya swallowed, refusing to let her fear show. "Maybe. But I think it's time someone brought those secrets into the light.

The man's eyes narrowed, and for a moment, Maya thought he might lunge across the table. But instead, he stood up, tossing a crumpled piece of paper onto the table. "If you're so determined, go ahead. Follow the trail. But don't say I didn't warn you."

He turned and walked out of the bar, leaving Maya alone with the paternal hastily scrawled address that led somewhere outside the city, deep into the foothills. She didn't know what was waiting for her there, but she was certain it was the final step in uncovering Lily's story.

Taking a deep breath, she slipped the paper into her bag. She was ready for whatever lay ahead.

5

The Trail in the Hills

The address on the crumpled piece of paper took Maya far from the bustling streets of downtown LA, leading her toward the foothills, where the city's noise faded into silence. As she drove, a sense of dread settled over her. She was leaving behind familiar territory, moving into the unknown, into the heart of the secrets surrounding Lily's death. But she couldn't stop now. Every instinct, every unanswered question, propelled her forward.

The sun was beginning to set as she reached a narrow, overgrown road that wound up into the hills. Her GPS had stopped working a mile back, and the address on the paper seemed to belong to a forgotten property, hidden away from prying eyes. She parked her car at the end of the road and continued foot, her senses on high alert, taking in the eerie quiet of the surroundings.

As she walked, she saw the faint outline of a building in the distance, half-hidden by dense trees and shrubs. It looked like an old, abandoned cabin, its windows dark and its walls weathered by time. The Rogue Guardians—or whoever this man worked for—had chosen the perfect place to hide whatever it was they didn't want the world to see.

Maya approached the cabin, her heart pounding as she reached the front door. She tested the handle, and to her surprise, it opened with a creak. The inside was dim, lit only by the fading light that seeped through cracks in the walls. Dust hung in the air, and the faint smell of mildew filled her nose.

She stepped inside, her footsteps echoing against the wooden floor. The cabin was bare, save for a few scattered objects, a broken chair, an empty bottle, a torn map pinned to the wall. She moved closer to the map, her fingers tracing over the faded markings. It seemed to outline a series of locations in the LA area, each marked with a symbol she didn't recognize. She took out her camera, snapping a photo, knowing she'd need time to make sense of this.

As she continued to explore, her flashlight beam caught on a small notebook lying in the corner of the room. She picked it up carefully, dusting off the cover. The pages were filled with hurried, scrawled handwriting, notes that seemed to jump from one thought to the next. She skimmed through, piecing together fragments:

"RG—meeting place, last Friday."

"Watched Echo Park girl, she suspects nothing."

"Too close to find out, keep her under control."

Maya's hands trembled as she read, the implications hitting her hard. The notebook confirmed that Lily had been followed, watched, monitored by this group—or person—who was desperate to keep her in line. They had planned every move, anticipating her reactions, all to stop her from uncovering something she shouldn't have known.

As she turned the page, she found a sketch of the same symbol she'd seen scratched onto the warehouse floor, a spiral surrounded by strange markings. Underneath it was written, "Guardian seal." Maya felt a chill run through her. This wasn't just a group; it was a network, something hidden and organized, bound by secrecy and ritual.

Suddenly, a noise outside broke the silent crackling of leaves, the sound of a footstep. Maya's heart leapt into her throat. She quickly tucked the notebook into her bag, her mind racing. She wasn't alone.

She shut off her flashlight, moving quietly toward a small window near the back of the cabin. Through the fading light, she could make out the figure of a man moving toward the cabin, his steps slow and deliberate. She recognized the silhouette instantly—the same man in the leather jacket, the one who had warned her at the bar. He was here, and she had no way out.

Maya's mind raced as she scanned the room, searching for a place to hide. She slipped behind a rotting wooden shelf, pressing herself against the wall and holding her breath. She heard the front door creak open, followed by the sound of footsteps entering the cabin. He moved through the room with an eerie calm, as if he knew exactly where to look, as if he could sense her presence.

"Curiosity's a dangerous thing, you know," he called out, his voice low and taunting. "You came all this way. Thought I'd at least congratulate you for that."

Maya swallowed, her heart pounding as she tightened her grip on her pepper spray. She wasn't sure how she could escape, but she was ready to defend herself if necessary. She peeked around the edge of the shelf, watching as he moved closer, his eyes scanning the room.

"I gave you every chance to walk away," he said, his voice laced with menace. "But you just had to keep digging, didn't you? People like you... always so eager to play the hero."

He stopped, his gaze landing on the torn map she'd been examining. He picked it up, a smirk playing on his lips. "Too bad you didn't figure out sooner that you're in over your head."

Maya's mind raced as she assessed her options. If she could just make it past him, she might have a chance to escape. She watched him carefully, waiting for the right moment, when his focus shifted back to the map. With a surge of adrenaline, she stepped out from behind the shelf and bolted toward the door.

But he was faster. He reached out, grabbing her arm and pulling her back with a force that sent her stumbling. She tried to raise her pepper spray, but he caught her wrist, twisting it just enough to make her drop the canister to the floor.

"Now, now," he said, his voice cold. "No need for that. We're just going to have a little talk."

Maya struggled against his grip, but he held her firmly, his expression unyielding. "I want to know what you think you're going to accomplish," he said, his voice soft and almost amused. "What do you think you're going to do? Expose us? Make the world care about one girl who went missing?"

"People do care," Maya shot back, her voice shaking. "And I'm going to make sure they know what you did to her."

He laughed, a dark, humorless sound. "You think anyone's going to listen to you? People go missing every day. Girls like Lily... they're disposable. No one's going to come looking, and no one's going to listen."

Maya's fear turned to anger, a white-hot rage coursing through her. She'd spent weeks uncovering every fragment of Lily's life, every moment she could salvage from the darkness. She knew Lily wasn't just "disposable." She was a person, someone with dreams, someone who deserved more than to be forgotten.

With a burst of strength, she twisted free of his grip, using her elbow to jab him hard in the ribs. He stumbled back, caught off guard, and Maya seized the opportunity, sprinting toward the door.

She dashed outside, her heart racing as she tore through the underbrush, branches scratching her skin as she ran. She could hear his footsteps behind her, his shouts growing louder as he pursued her down the hillside. But she didn't stop, didn't look back. She pushed herself forward, her only thought to get away, to make it back to safety.

After what felt like an eternity, she reached the road, her legs burning as she sprinted toward her car. She jumped inside, slamming the door and locking it just as she saw him emerge from the trees, his face twisted in anger. She didn't waste a second, turning the key in the ignition and speeding away, her heart pounding as she left the cabin—and him—behind.

Back at Her Apartment

Once home, Maya bolted the door and leaned against it, her whole body shaking. She took out the notebook she'd grabbed from the cabin, flipping through the pages with trembling hands. She had enough now—enough to tell Lily's story, to expose the network of secrecy and silence that had led to her death.

The notebook, the photos, the map—they were all pieces of a puzzle, evidence that could finally reveal the truth about the Rogue Guardians and the shadowy figure who had tried to keep it buried. She could feel the weight of it, the story that would finally bring Lily's life and death into the light.

She sat down at her desk, opening her laptop and beginning to type, her fingers moving swiftly as she crafted Lily's story, every detail raw and unfiltered. She was done hiding, done being afraid. She would share what she'd discovered, even if it meant risking everything.

As she typed, she realized this wasn't just Lily's story anymore, it was her own. A story about courage, about refusing to stay silent in the face of darkness, about fighting to make the world remember those who might otherwise be forgotten.

And as she finished the first chapter, she knew that no matter what happened next, she had finally given Lily the voice she'd been denied.

6

Unmasking the Shadows

Maya barely slept that night, her mind racing with everything she had learned. The Rogue Guardians, the mysterious man, the danger she'd barely escaped in the cabin—all of it felt surreal, like she'd stumbled into a world hidden in plain sight. But the notebook she'd taken from the cabin was real, filled with entries that pointed to something far larger than she'd first imagined. The Rogue Guardians weren't just a random group; they were an organization, one whose reach extended beyond Echo Park and the streets of LA.

When morning came, she opened her laptop, determined to dig deeper. If she was going to expose the truth, she needed more than just fragmented notes and her own account. She needed connections, names, patterns that would prove Lily's story was part of something bigger. So, she combed through the notebook, this time meticulously analyzing each word, each phrase, looking for clues.

In the margins of one page, she found an address, barely legible and hastily scrawled. The address was followed by the phrase, "Contact: The Archivist." Maya didn't know who "The Archivist" was, but she had a strong feeling this lead would take her closer to the heart of the Rogue Guardians.

Later That Day

Maya arrived at the address in the afternoon. It was a nondescript building on the outskirts of downtown LA, nestled between an old bookstore and a pawnshop. The place looked like it had been abandoned for years, its windows covered in dust, and the paint on the door was chipped and peeling. But as Maya approached, she noticed a faint glow coming from inside, a soft light seeping through a crack in the door.

She knocked, her heart pounding as she waited. Moments later, the door creaked open, revealing a thin man in his sixties, with sharp eyes behind a pair of round glasses. He looked at her with an unreadable expression, his gaze flicking to the notebook she held in her hands.

"You're not one of them," he said, his voice low and wary.

Maya shook her head, holding up the notebook. "I'm not. But I found this, and I think you might know what it means. I'm looking for answers. About the Rogue Guardians, and about a girl named Lily."

The man's eyes softened, though his expression remained guarded. "Come in," he said, stepping aside to let her enter. The room was dimly lit, filled with old books, stacks of files, and boxes labeled with strange symbols. He led her to a table piled high with papers, motioning for her to sit.

"I'm The Archivist," he said, settling into a chair across from her. "I was once part of the Rogue Guardians... until I realized what they truly were. Now I keep records—evidence of the things they try to hide."

Maya felt a surge of relief. Finally, she was speaking to someone who understood, someone who could give her the context she so desperately needed. She showed him the notebook, pointing to the entries about Lily, about the spiral symbol, and about the man who had been following her.

The Archivist leaned over the notebook; his face grim as he read. "The spiral is a symbol of binding," he explained. "It's a mark they use to track those they consider 'threats'—anyone who might expose their secrets. The Rogue Guardians claim they're protecting the city, that they're the unseen keepers of balance. But in truth, they manipulate, blackmail, and silence anyone who threatens to disrupt their power."

Maya's stomach turned as she listened. "And Lily?" she asked softly. "Why were they following her?"

The Archivist sighed, his gaze distant. "I remember her. She came to one of their events, hoping to get involved, to find community. But she saw too much. She overheard something she shouldn't have, something about their more... illegal operations. When they realized she knew, they couldn't let her go."

Maya's heart broke for Lily, imagining her as a hopeful young girl who had come to LA looking for connection, only to be ensnared in a web of secrecy and danger. "They killed her, didn't they?" she asked, her voice trembling.

The Archivist nodded; his expression was sorrowful. "Yes. They framed it as an accident, but it was calculated. They couldn't risk her exposing them. It's what they do—anyone who threatens the group's existence is removed."

Maya clenched her fists, anger and sorrow churning inside her. "I need to expose them," she said, her voice filled with determination. "People need to know what they did to her. They need to know who the Rogue Guardians really are."

The Archivist looked at her, a flicker of respect in his eyes. "You're brave, but you're also in danger. They're already watching you, and if you get too close, they won't hesitate to do the same to you as they did to Lily."

Maya felt a chill, but she refused to back down. "I don't care. She deserves justice. And if I don't do this, no one will."

The Archivist studied her for a moment, then nodded. "I can help. I have files and records that I've kept hidden. Evidence of their operations, their members, their network. If we can compile it, we can bring them down. But you'll have to be careful. They have eyes everywhere."

Maya agreed, and they spent hours going through his records, pulling together every piece of evidence they could find. The files were a treasure trove of information—names, locations, photographs of clandestine meetings, documents detailing illegal activities. It was more than enough to expose the Rogue Guardians, more than enough to finally give Lily justice.

As they worked, Maya felt a surge of hope. For the first time, she could see a way forward, a way to honor Lily's memory and ensure that no one else would suffer the same fate.

That Night

Maya returned to her apartment, exhausted but filled with a sense of purpose. She had everything she needed to write Lily's story, to shine a light on the darkness that had taken her life. She began typing, pouring her heart into every word, weaving together the pieces of Lily's life, her dreams, her tragic death, and the hidden world of the Rogue Guardians.

But just as she finished the first draft, her phone buzzed with a message. She picked it up, feeling a familiar chill as she read the text.

We know what you're doing. Stop, or there will be consequences.

Maya's hand shook, but she took a deep breath, her resolve unshaken. She was past the point of fear. She replied simply: I'm not afraid of you.

Then she closed her laptop, saving her work, and prepared for the next steps. She knew the Rogue Guardians wouldn't go down without a fight, but she was ready. With the Archivist's help, she had a plan in place to distribute the files, to get the truth out into the world, no matter what the cost.

As she lay in bed that night, her mind still racing, she felt an unexpected sense of peace. Lily's story will finally be told. Her memory would live on, and her voice would not be silenced. And for the first time, Maya felt she was exactly where she was meant to be—standing on the edge of the truth, unafraid to step into the light.

7

The Truth Unleashed

Maya woke before dawn, her mind focused and clear. Today was the day she'd released everything. She'd spent the night crafting an article that told Lily's story in heartbreaking, raw detail, complete with the Rogue Guardians' secrets that The Archivist had helped her uncover. She was ready to send it to every major news outlet, blog, and social media platform she could reach.

The files from The Archivist were uploaded to a secure server, and she'd arranged a timed release, just in case anything happened to her. It was a final layer of security, a way to ensure that the truth would come out, even if the Rogue Guardians tried to stop her.

As the first rays of sunlight filtered into her apartment, Maya sent the article to her contact list, then posted a link to the files on every platform she could think of. Her hands trembled as she hit "publish," knowing that there was no turning back.

Almost immediately, her phone began to buzz with notifications. Messages flooded in from friends, acquaintances, and strangers, all responding to the explosive information she'd shared. The Rogue Guardians' name was already beginning to spread, people sharing the story and expressing outrage. The organization had been operating in the shadows for too long, and now, finally, the light was shining on their secrets.

Later That Morning

Maya stayed indoors, watching the reaction online as the story spread. News outlets picked it up quickly, each one amplifying Lily's story and the organization behind her death. She knew this would rattle the Rogue Guardians; their careful web of secrecy was being ripped apart, and they wouldn't be able to stop the spread of the truth.

Her phone buzzed again, this time with a text from The Archivist: "They know it's out. They're scrambling. Be careful—don't let your guard down."

Maya felt a surge of adrenaline. She knew she was risking everything, but for the first time, she felt truly powerful. She'd given Lily a voice, one that echoed louder than any threat.

Moments later, there was a knock on her door. Her pulse spiked as she approached cautiously, peering through the peephole. It was a man in a suit, his expression calm yet tense. Maya's hand hovered over her phone, ready to call for help, but something told her to open the door and face him.

She unlocked the door, opening it just enough to see his face clearly. "Can I help you?"

The man held up a badge, identifying himself as a detective with the LAPD. "Miss Patel? We received an anonymous tip regarding the information you've been sharing. May I come in?"

Maya hesitated but ultimately let him in, her curiosity winning over her caution. She led him to her living room, where he sat down, his gaze steady and professional.

"First of all," he began, "thank you for coming forward with this information. I know it must have taken courage."

Maya nodded, her heart racing. "I didn't think anyone would believe me."

The detective looked at her with a mix of admiration and seriousness. "Believe me, you're not the only one who's encountered the Rogue Guardians. We've been tracking them for years, but they're experts at covering their tracks. Until now, we haven't had enough evidence to pursue them directly."

Maya felt a sense of relief, realizing that she wasn't alone in this fight. "So… what happens now?"

He leaned forward, his expression resolute. "Now, we use everything you've gathered to bring them down. We'll open an official investigation, follow the leads you've provided, and connect with former members who might be willing to testify. Your actions have given us the break we needed."

A wave of relief washed over her, but it was tempered by a lingering unease. "What about their threats?" she asked, her voice barely a whisper. "They've been watching me. They already tried to—"

He raised a hand, reassuring her. "We'll place you under protective watch. They're dangerous, but they're on the defensive now. This exposure has weakened their control, and that's when they're most vulnerable.

Maya nodded, her mind racing with the possibilities. The police were involved. The public knew. For the first time, the Rogue Guardians would be held accountable, and Lily's death would not be forgotten.

That Night

As the news spread, Maya's story reached millions. Social media exploded with the hashtag #JusticeForLily, and people from across the country voiced their outrage, demanding accountability. The Rogue Guardians, once hidden and powerful, were now the subject of intense public scrutiny. Former members came forward with their own stories, detailing the manipulation and control they'd endured. The organization's influence was crumbling, piece by piece.

Maya spent the night scrolling through the responses, overwhelmed by the support pouring in. People sent her messages of gratitude, calling her a hero, a voice for the voiceless. She felt a strange sense of peace, knowing that she had done what Lily couldn't have told her story.

But as the night wore on, a deep exhaustion settled over her. The weight of everything she'd been through, every threat, every moment of fear, began to sink in. She closed her laptop and lay down, letting herself feel the full weight of her journey. She had done what she set out to do, but the scars of the experience would remain.

A Week Later

The days that followed were a blur of interviews, police meetings, and press coverage. Maya's life was suddenly public, her name tied to one of the most explosive stories in recent history. The LAPD's investigation into the Rogue Guardians was officially underway, with former members providing testimony and evidence to dismantle the organization from the inside.

Then, one morning, Maya received a letter in her mailbox. It was handwritten, the envelope unmarked. She opened it cautiously, her heart pounding as she read the words inside:

"You did what I couldn't. Thank you for giving me peace. —L"

A shiver ran through her as she reread the message. It was impossible, but somehow, she felt Lily's presence in those words, as if she had reached out from beyond, offering gratitude and closure. Maya tucked the letter into her journal, a quiet smile on her face. She'd given Lily a voice, and in doing so, had found her own.

8

The Last Goodbye

It had been several months since the trial and the dismantling of the Rogue Guardians, but for Maya, the experience lingered in her mind like an indelible mark. She had continued her work as a journalist, focusing on cases that highlighted injustice, using her platform to bring awareness to those who needed it. But no story, no case, held the same weight in her heart as Lily's.

On a cool autumn morning, Maya found herself drawn back to Echo Park. The air was crisp, the sun filtering through the trees, casting a gentle glow over the lake. She hadn't been back here since the investigation had ended, but something within her had called her back, like a final chapter waiting to be closed.

She walked slowly along the familiar paths, her feet tracing the same steps she had taken all those months ago. She paused by the bench where she'd first seen Lily, feeling a wave of emotions rush over her—grief, triumph, and a profound sense of connection. This was the place where it had all started, and where it felt like it was ending too.

As she sat down, she took out the letter she had received, Lily's final message that had somehow, impossibly, made its way to her. She ran her fingers over the words, feeling a quiet sense of closure, she hadn't expected. There was something comforting knowing that Lily's spirit had found peace, that her voice had been heard.

A quiet voice interrupted her thoughts.

"Excuse me," said an older woman, her expression warm and curious. "Are you the journalist? The one who told that girl's story?"

Maya looked up, a gentle smile spreading across her face. "Yes, that's me."

The woman sat down beside her, gazing out over the lake. "I was here the day they found her. Poor thing. I didn't know her, but I always thought about her, wondered if anyone would remember her. She turned to Maya, her eyes soft. "Thank you for giving her a story."

Maya nodded, feeling a surge of gratitude. "She deserved to be remembered. She deserved justice."

The woman patted her hand gently. "You did a good thing. It's rare to find people who care enough to fight like that."

They sat in silence for a while, the sounds of the park filling the space between them. When the woman left, Maya stayed, letting the memories of her journey with Lily wash over her. She'd found strength in Lily's story, and in the process, she had discovered her own voice, her own purpose. She had fought not just for Lily, but for every person who had ever been silent.

After a while, Maya stood and walked to the lake's edge. She took a deep breath, feeling the weight of the past finally lift from her shoulders. She took out her camera, capturing the scene one last time, as if preserving the final piece of a memory she would carry with her always.

Weeks Later

Back in her apartment, Maya finished editing the last of her notes and photographs, compiling them into a book about the journey she had taken with Lily. She titled it Voices Unheard: The Story of Lily and the Fight for Justice, dedicating it to Lily and to everyone who had been silenced by those in power. It was a labor of love, her way of ensuring Lily's memory would live on, inspiring others to find the courage to speak up.

The book was published quietly, but it began to gain attention, readers captivated by the raw honesty of the story, the courage of a young girl who had faced a hidden evil, and the determination of a journalist who wouldn't let her be forgotten. Messages poured in from people who had been affected by the book, who had felt inspired to fight their own battles, to seek their own justice.

One night, Maya received an unexpected email from a young woman who had been in a similar situation to Lily. The message was simple, but it moved her deeply:

"Thank you for telling her story. I felt like I wasn't alone."

Maya replied, knowing that Lily's legacy had found its way into the hearts of those who needed it most. It was a quiet victory, one that filled her with peace.

9

Shadows Cast Wider

Maya's life had changed dramatically since her book was published. Voices Unheard had gone from a quiet release to a bestseller, praised for its raw portrayal of courage in the face of corruption. Her story about Lily had struck a chord, inspiring countless readers to speak out about their own experiences with injustice. But with her newfound fame came unexpected scrutiny, pressure, and a feeling that she was being watched more closely than ever.

As the weeks went on, the media requests, public appearances, and interviews kept her busy, pulling her into a whirlwind she hadn't anticipated. Every story, every testimony she heard from those who reached out to her, deepened her understanding of the impact Lily's story had. Yet Maya couldn't shake the lingering feeling that the story wasn't truly over, that the Rogue Guardians—or perhaps something larger—was still watching her every move.

One morning, as she sat in her apartment, sifting through the latest batch of emails, a message caught her eye. The subject line was simple: We need to talk—urgent. The sender's name was unrecognizable, and there were no attachments. Usually, she might have dismissed it as spam, but her instincts told her otherwise. She clicked it open and read:

"I know the truth about the Rogue Guardians. There's more to their story than you've uncovered. If you want to know what really happened to Lily—and what could happen to you—you'll meet me tonight. Echo Park, 11 PM."

Maya's heart skipped a beat. Was this someone who had been part of the Rogue Guardians? A former member? Or was this a trap, a final attempt to silence her for good? She reread the email, her mind racing. If there was more to Lily's story, she had to know. But she also knew that going to Echo Park alone at night could be a dangerous choice.

Later That Evening

Despite her fear, Maya decided to go. She arrived at Echo Park just before 11 PM, the lake glistening under the moonlight, the familiar paths now shadowed and still. She kept her phone close, her finger hovering over the emergency call button as she scanned the area for any sign of her mysterious contact.

As she waited, her mind wandered to Lily, to the girl whose story had changed everything. Maya had told her story to the world, but somehow, tonight, it felt as if she were stepping into it. She was in the very place where Lily had once spent her final days, haunted by the people who wanted to silence her.

A figure appeared on the path, emerging from the shadows. He was older, in his fifties, his face weathered and wary. He wore a long coat, his hands buried deep in his pockets as he approached her. Maya tensed but held her ground.

"You must be Maya," he said, his voice low and gravelly.

Maya nodded, trying to mask her unease. "And you are?"

He hesitated, glancing around before he answered. "Call me Richard. I used to be one of them—a Rogue Guardian. But that was a long time ago."

Maya's eyes narrowed, studying his face, looking for any sign of deception. "Why should I believe you?"

He let out a bitter laugh, his gaze distant. "I don't expect you to. I've kept silent for years, pretending it was all behind me. But your book... it stirred up memories I'd tried to bury. And after I read it, I realized there was something I needed to tell you. Lily's death wasn't just about what she overheard. She was onto something far bigger."

Maya's heart raced. "What do you mean?"

He took a step closer, his eyes dark with fear and regret. "The Rogue Guardians were only a front. They were used to keep people like me in line; to make us believe we were doing something meaningful, protecting the city. But we were just pawns. There's an organization above them—an invisible hand controlling everything. They don't care about justice. They care about control. And anyone who gets close to their secrets... doesn't last long."

Maya felt a chill run through her. "Are you saying Lily uncovered something about them? Something that got her killed?"

Richard nodded slowly. "Yes. And if you're not careful, you'll be next."

The Revelation

As they talked, Richard told her about a network that extended far beyond the Rogue Guardians. He spoke of hidden deals, bribes to government officials, and connections to people in high places who used the Guardians as a convenient cover. Lily, he explained, had somehow stumbled onto evidence of this larger conspiracy—proof that could bring the whole network down. And she wasn't the only one. Others who had tried to expose it had disappeared, just like her.

Maya felt a rising sense of dread. The Rogue Guardians had been dangerous enough, but this was something much larger, much darker than she'd imagined. She had thought her investigation was over, that she had found justice for Lily. But now she realized she'd only scratched the surface.

Richard handed her a small flash drive, his hand trembling. "This is all I could gather before I got out. I kept it hidden, in case I ever needed proof. But I'm done running. If they come for me, so be it. But you... you have a chance to finish what Lily started."

Maya took the flash drive, brushing her fingers against him. "Why now? Why tell me this after all these years?"

He looked away, his expression haunted. "Because I was too much of a coward to do it myself. And because... Lily deserves to be remembered for what she tried to do, not just for how she died."

Before Maya could respond, he turned and walked away, disappearing into the shadows as quickly as he had come. She stood there for a long moment, staring at the flash drive in her hand, her mind reeling from everything he had revealed. This was bigger than she'd ever imagined. If she went forward with this, it would mean uncovering a network of corruption that could reach the highest levels.

Back at Her Apartment

Maya returned home, her mind racing as she plugged the flash drive into her computer. Files, reports, and encrypted documents filled her screen. She scanned through them, her heart pounding as she saw names, transactions, and emails connecting powerful people to a web of manipulation and control. Lily had been right—she had uncovered something that went beyond the Rogue Guardians, something that threatened the very fabric of the justice system.

Maya felt both exhilarated and terrified. She knew that publishing this information would be dangerous, that it would put her in even more jeopardy than before. But if she didn't tell this story, if she let Lily's discovery die in silence, then everything she had fought for would be in vain.

She took a deep breath, steadying herself as she began to compile the files, organizing the information into a new article. This time, she knew she'd have to be even more careful. The people she was dealing with were more powerful than the Rogue Guardians, and they wouldn't hesitate to eliminate her if they thought she was a threat.

As dawn approached, Maya finished the article, saving it to multiple secure drives, preparing it for release. She was ready to publish it, but she knew she'd need allies—journalists, activists, people she could trust to help protect her and spread the truth.

Just as she was about to reach out to her contacts, her phone buzzed. It was a message from an unknown number.

"We warned you. Last chance to walk away."

Maya felt a surge of defiance as she read the message. She was in deeper than she had ever intended, but she couldn't turn back now. Lily's voice, her memory, her fight, they were all a part of her, and Maya was determined to see this through.

With a deep breath, she hit "send," releasing her findings to a trusted network of journalists and activists, ensuring that the story would spread far and wide, beyond the reach of those who wanted it silenced.

She knew the storm was coming, that the fight ahead would be more dangerous than anything she'd faced before. But as the first light of dawn filled her apartment, Maya felt a fierce, unbreakable resolve. She had become more than just a journalist; she was now a voice for justice, an ally to those who had none, and a force that could no longer be silenced.

And as she watched her story begin to ripple across the internet, Maya knew she wasn't alone. She felt Lily's presence, quietly guiding her forward, reminding her that sometimes, the truth was worth any price.

10

Into the Crosshairs

The days following Maya's latest article were a blur. The exposé spread faster than she had anticipated, sparking outrage, support, and an immediate demand for investigations. Journalists from major outlets began reaching out to her, seeking more information about the elusive network she'd uncovered. Public figures voiced their shock, calling for transparency, while the online world buzzed with theories, speculations, and a new hashtag: Expose the Network.

Yet Maya's victory felt tenuous. She knew she had thrown herself headfirst into a deeper and darker world, one that went beyond the Rogue Guardians. The people she had exposed wielded significant power, and they wouldn't take this lightly. The warning texts were constant now, each one more ominous than the last. But she refused to let them intimidate her.

Her apartment, usually a sanctuary, now felt more like a bunker. She kept the curtains drawn, her phone close, her laptop secure. She'd even taken to staying at a friend's place on some nights, moving carefully to avoid drawing any attention.

On her fifth night after publishing, Maya received a call from The Archivist.

"They know, Maya," he said, his voice strained. "They know you've got their files, and they're not happy. I'm hearing things… you need to be more careful than ever."

Maya took a shaky breath, her pulse quickening. "What do you mean, 'hearing things?'"

The Archivist paused, then spoke in a hushed tone. "They've activated what they call the 'Retrievers'—agents sent to silence anyone who threatens the network. They're ruthless, and they're already tracking your movements. You need to get somewhere safe. Now."

A chill ran down her spine. The name "Retrievers" sounded ominous enough, but the Archivist's tone made it worse. He knew what these people were capable of, and the fear in his voice was unlike anything she'd ever heard.

"Where should I go?" she asked, forcing herself to remain calm.

"Leave LA. I have a contact who can help you. Meet me at the safe house. I'll send the coordinates," he said, and before she could ask anything more, he hung up.

The Escape

Maya packed quickly, taking only the essentials: her laptop, the flash drives, a change of clothes, and some cash. She was nervous, checking the windows every few minutes, her paranoia amplifying every sound outside. She left through the back entrance, her heart pounding as she made her way to her car, keeping her head low, scanning her surroundings. The streets were empty, but she couldn't shake the feeling that eyes were on her.

Following The Archivist's instructions, she drove out of LA, heading north on a secluded route to avoid any main roads. She could almost feel her fear turning into adrenaline, fueling her forward. She wouldn't let them stop her. Lily's story, the network's secrets, she had to keep them safe, no matter what.

Hours Later: The Safe House

The coordinates led her to a remote cabin tucked into the woods, well outside the reach of city lights. The Archivist was waiting for her, looking more haggard than she remembered. He wore a heavy coat, his expression grim as he waved at her inside. The cabin was small and sparse, furnished with little more than a table, a few chairs, and a cot in the corner. A single lamp casts a warm glow, making the place feel strangely secure, like a haven hidden from the world.

"They won't find you here," he said, his voice low. "At least, not yet."

Maya sat down, feeling the weight of the past few days crash over her. "What is this network, really?" she asked, her voice barely a whisper. "How far does it go?"

The Archivist sighed, leaning back in his chair. "Farther than even, I know. They control information, influence powerful people, and manipulate markets. They built the Rogue Guardians to maintain control in LA, but they've done it in other cities too. Their reach is wide, but their strength is in secrecy. No one outside the organization knows the full extent of what they do."

Maya shivered. "And Lily... she was just one person who got too close."

"Exactly," he replied, his eyes sad. "She wasn't the first, and she won't be the last. But you... you're different. You've already exposed part of their structure. They're scrambling now, but they'll do everything they can to make sure you don't go any further."

Maya clenched her fists. "Then we go further," she said, her voice firm. "We gather everything we can, piece together their connections, their assets. We've come this far—if we stop now, they'll just bury everything again."

The Archivist looked at her, admiration and a hint of fear in his eyes. "You're braver than I thought. But this will be dangerous. If we do this, there's no going back."

Maya met his gaze, unwavering. "I've already crossed that line."

The Investigation Deepens

For the next week, Maya and The Archivist worked tirelessly, piecing together clues from the files. She learned of high-profile politicians, business moguls, and even law enforcement officers who were tangled in the network's web. Each new connection was a revelation, a piece of a puzzle that seemed both daunting and horrifying.

One night, while sifting through the files, Maya stumbled upon a name she recognized: a prominent investigative journalist who had disappeared years ago under mysterious circumstances. She remembered reading about the case—he'd been known for exposing corporate corruption, and his disappearance had left a huge void in the field.

"The network got to him, didn't they?" she asked The Archivist, showing him the name on the screen.

The Archivist nodded; his expression grim. "He was one of their first targets. They're meticulous. Anyone who crosses them, anyone who threatens their control, disappears. That's how they keep their secrets buried."

Maya felt a shiver run down her spine. She was following in the footsteps of people who had tried and failed to take down this organization. But she couldn't let fear stop her. She'd already come too far, and she knew that every discovery she made brought her closer to the heart of the network.

A New Ally

One evening, as she was reviewing files, she received an encrypted message from an anonymous contact. The message was brief but intriguing:

"I have information. I used to work for them. If you're serious about bringing them down, meet me tomorrow. Location to follow."

Maya's instincts told her it could be a trap, but it was also possible this person could be the ally they needed. The Archivist was hesitant, but Maya convinced him. "We must take the chance. If this person is real, they could have intel we'd never get otherwise."

The next day, she went to the meeting point—a secluded café in a small town just outside the city. She took a seat in the back, her gaze constantly scanning the room, looking for anyone who seemed suspicious.

A woman approached, sliding into the seat across from her. She looked at Maya's age, with sharp eyes and a cautious demeanor. She introduced herself only as "Jules."

"I know you've been looking into them," Jules said quietly. "I was part of their operations team, managing communications. I left when I realized what they were really doing, but I've been in hiding ever since."

Maya leaned in, her heart pounding. "Why come forward now?"

Jules hesitated, glancing around before speaking. "Because I saw your article. I saw what you did for that girl, Lily. I thought I was alone in this, but you've already exposed them more than I ever thought possible. I want to help, if you'll let me."

Maya felt a surge of hope. "We could use your help. I have files, connections we're piecing together, but it's hard to know who to trust."

Jules nodded. "I can give you their inner structure—the names of key players, details of their safehouses, how they communicate. They're careful, but they've gotten sloppy in recent years. We might be able to use that against them."

The Plan

With Jules's insider knowledge and The Archivist's files, Maya formulated a plan. They would release the remaining evidence, targeting key figures within the network, using timed releases and multiple channels to ensure the information couldn't be suppressed. They set up secure backups in case anything went wrong, each piece of data connected to a web of contacts who could continue the fight if something happened to them.

But as they prepared to launch the final phase, Maya received one last warning. A message from an anonymous number flashed on her screen:

"We know where you are. This is your last chance to stop. Next time, you won't be so lucky."

She showed the message to The Archivist and Jules, her resolve only hardening. "It's too late for them to intimidate us," she said, her voice steady. "They wanted to keep people like Lily quiet, to keep people like us afraid. But we're not afraid anymore."

And as she hit the button to release the first wave of files, Maya knew she was ready to face whatever came next. She'd uncovered the network, she'd given Lily's story the justice it deserved, and now she was ready to stand up to the shadows that had loomed over her life—and over countless others—for far too long.

11

Striking the Core

The files went live just before dawn. Maya had crafted a series of timed releases that would drop every hour, each one revealing another layer of the network's corruption. By the morning sun broke over the horizon, her exposé had already begun to gain traction. Journalists, activists, and even some politicians were sharing the information across their platforms, using Maya's work to call for an official investigation.

Maya knew this was a point of no return. The network's leaders would be desperate to silence her, and the threats would only escalate. But now she had allies—The Archivist, Jules, and the public who were rallying around the story. She was no longer fighting alone.

That Morning

Maya, The Archivist, and Jules sat around a small table in the safe house, monitoring the story's spread from multiple devices. Jules was calm but focused, her eyes scanning the screens as she tracked the impact of each timed release.

"Their structure's unraveling faster than I thought," Jules remarked. "I've seen some of the higher-ups starting to panic—they're already trying to scrub their digital footprints."

The Archivist shook his head. "Too little, too late. They never thought anyone would get this far, but now they're in the spotlight.

Maya felt a mix of triumph and anxiety. She had spent so many months fearing this moment, yet now she felt oddly calm. She knew she'd done everything possible to ensure the story couldn't be silent. The network's secrets were exposed, and there was no way to undo that.

Suddenly, her phone buzzed with a new message from an unknown number:

"You can't win this war, Maya. You're out of your league."

Her jaw clenched. The network was grasping at straws, throwing out threats they hoped would scare her into submission. She shared the message with Jules, who only smirked.

"They're the ones out of their league," Jules said, her voice filled with defiance. "We have the truth on our side, and the world is watching now."

Afternoon: A New Revelation

The story continued to spread, gaining more visibility with each passing hour. Media outlets picked up the files, and soon, news stations across the country were discussing the Rogue Guardians and the larger network behind them. People were outraged, demanding accountability, and many public officials who were tied to the network began to face intense scrutiny. Some even resigned, unable to withstand the backlash.

But then, something unexpected happened. A high-profile politician, Senator Charles Kingston, publicly announced his affiliation with the network. He was a known advocate for corporate reform and government transparency, which made his admission more shocking. In a televised press conference, Kingston denied any knowledge of the organization's darker dealings, claiming he had been involved for altruistic reasons, believing the group was a coalition focused on maintaining civic order.

"This isn't the organization you think it is," Kingston said, his face pale and drawn. "I'm not the only one who's been deceived. I was told the Rogue Guardians were a positive force for change, ensuring stability in uncertain times. But if what's being revealed is true, then I was lied to, just like the rest of you."

Maya, watching the press conference with Jules and The Archivist, felt her anger rise. She knew that Kingston's confession was a half-truth at best. He might have joined under that pretense, but he had stayed long enough to understand the network's real purpose. Still, his admission was a breakthrough crack in the armor that might encourage other members to come forward, either to save face or to shift blame.

"This could work in our favor," Jules said thoughtfully. "If more of them start confessing, we'll have a clearer map of the network's structure. And they'll implicate each other in the process."

The Archivist nodded. "It's a domino effect. Once one falls, the rest will follow."

Nightfall: The Final Push

As evening approached, the pressure on Maya intensified. More messages flooded her inbox, some from anonymous contacts with new leaders, others from people she didn't know, pleading for her to expose other organizations they claimed were connected to the network.

One email stood out. It was from an encrypted address, and the message contained a simple but urgent request:

"There's more you haven't uncovered. They have another base of operations in the city warehouse near the docks. You'll find the core team there. But you must act fast."

Maya shared the email with Jules and The Archivist. "Could this be real?" she asked, her voice filled with cautious hope.

Jules's face turned serious. "It's possible. The network often has contingency plans, hidden locations where they store backup records. If this tip is legitimate, that warehouse could contain critical information."

The Archivist looked grim. "But it's a risk. If it's a trap, it could be their way of drawing you out, away from the public eye."

Maya considered her options. She knew this was dangerous, but if there was any chance of finding more evidence, she had to take it. Every piece of information they gathered weakened the network further, and if she could find something decisive, it could be the final nail in the coffin.

"I'll go," she said, determination hardening her voice. "But I'll need your help to ensure that, if anything happens to me, the story keeps going."

Jules nodded, her eyes flashing with resolve. "We'll back you up. But be careful, Maya. They'll do anything to stop you."

At the Warehouse

That night, Maya arrived at the warehouse by the docks, her heart pounding with a mix of fear and adrenaline. She had told Jules and The Archivist to monitor her location remotely, and she wore a hidden recording device to capture any evidence she found. She crept through the shadows, every sense heightened as she scanned the area.

The warehouse was massive, its walls covered in faded graffiti, its windows dark. She made her way to a side entrance, slipping inside quietly. The interior was dimly lit, and the air smelled of dust and mildew. Rows of file cabinets and storage crates lined the walls, and in the center of the room, a large table was scattered with papers, laptops, and what looked like surveillance equipment.

As Maya moved closer, she began rifling through the files on the table, snapping photos of documents that referenced the network's operations and connections. She found a list of names—more politicians, business leaders, even a few journalists—people who were either members or complicit in the network's activities.

Suddenly, she heard footsteps approaching from the far end of the warehouse. She froze, her heart pounding as she ducked behind a stack of crates, clutching her phone tightly.

Two men entered the room, their faces obscured in the shadows. One of them was speaking in a low, urgent tone. "We need to relocate everything tonight. That journalist has already done too much damage. If she gets her hands on these files, it's over."

Maya's heart raced. She recognized the voice—it was one of the network's top operatives, someone she had come across in her research but never thought she'd meet in person.

The second man spoke, his tone bitter. "The higher-ups are furious. They want her taken care of. They're saying we may need to use... extreme measures."

Maya's blood ran cold. She stayed perfectly still, holding her breath as the men continued their conversation.

"We'll burn this place down if we have to," the first man said. "No evidence, no witnesses."

Maya realized she had only moments to act. She quickly texted Jules and The Archivist, alerting them to the situation. Then, taking a deep breath, she activated her recording device, letting it capture the men's voices and their damning words.

But as she shifted her weight, her foot brushed against a metal rod on the floor, sending it clattering across the concrete. The noise echoed through the warehouse, and the men immediately froze.

"Who's there?" one of them shouted, his voice filled with suspicion.

Maya's heart pounded as she ducked lower, trying to stay hidden. But the men were already moving in her direction, their footsteps growing louder.

Realizing she had no other choice, Maya bolted from her hiding spot, sprinting toward the exit. The men shouted behind her, and she could hear their footsteps thundering as they gave chase. She pushed herself faster, her lungs burning as she raced through the warehouse and out into the cold night air.

She didn't stop running until she was far from the warehouse, her breaths ragged as she finally slowed down. She had escaped—but she knew that the chase had only just begun.

Back at the Safe House

When she returned, Jules and The Archivist were waiting for her, their faces filled with relief and concern.

"What happened?" Jules asked, her eyes wide.

Maya took a deep breath, replaying the recorded audio for them. As the men's voices filled the room, detailing their plans to "take care" of her and eliminate the evidence, a grim silence settled over them.

"This is it," The Archivist said, his voice barely a whisper. "This is the evidence we needed. Their threat, their willingness to destroy everything, even people—just to protect their secrets. This will be the final blow."

Maya nodded, exhaustion and determination mixing in equal measure. She knew the danger was far from over, but with this new evidence, they had the power to expose the full extent of the network's operations and its ruthlessness.

They prepared to release the audio along with the final files, ready to face whatever consequences awaited them. Maya felt a sense of fierce satisfaction. She was ready for the battle that lay ahead, knowing that this time, the truth was on her side—and nothing could silence it.

12

The World Watching

The release of the audio recording hit the media like a thunderclap. Within hours, news outlets, bloggers, and social media erupted with damning evidence. For the first time, the public had indisputable proof of the network's ruthlessness and its willingness to destroy anyone who stood in its way. The names in Maya's files and recordings implicated prominent figures, and suddenly, people who had once been untouchable were scrambling to justify their involvement or distance themselves from the organization.

Despite the triumph of the exposé, Maya felt an underlying tension. She knew the network wasn't done yet. They wouldn't let this go without a fight. And now, with the truth out in the open, she had become their primary target.

Later That Day

Maya, The Archivist, and Jules gathered at the safe house, reviewing the fallout from the latest release. Jules scanned news alerts and social media while The Archivist quietly sorted through the remaining files, occasionally nodding in approval at the online chaos they had unleashed.

"They're already panicking," Jules said, a hint of satisfaction in her voice. "High-ranking members are turning on each other, and the media is eating it up. We've done more damage in a week than they ever expected."

Maya nodded, but she couldn't shake a feeling of unease. "This is good, but it's also when they'll be at their most desperate. We're close to taking them down completely, but they're not going to go quietly."

Just then, her phone buzzed off with an incoming call from an unknown number. Maya hesitated, glancing at The Archivist and Jules, before answering. She put the phone on the speaker.

"Hello?"

A voice came through, calm but menacing. "Miss Patel, you've been quite busy. We didn't expect you to have such… perseverance."

Maya felt her pulse quicken, but she held her ground. "You should have. Did you think you could silence everyone forever?"

The voice laughed softly. "Perhaps we underestimated your resolve. But you've left us no choice. We can't allow someone like you to continue disrupting our operations. Walk away now, and you'll be spared. If you don't... well, I'm sure you understand the consequences."

Jules leaned toward the phone; her voice filled with defiance. "We're not afraid of you. The world's already watching, and they're not going to look away now."

There was a pause, and then the voice spoke again, colder this time. "You're mistaken if you think the world will protect you. They'll forget soon enough. And when they do, we'll still be here."

The line went dead, and Maya set her phone down, her hand trembling slightly. She looked up at her friends, fierce determination burning in her eyes. "They're bluffing. They're just trying to scare us into backing down."

The Archivist nodded, but his expression was grave. "They're scared, yes, but desperate people are dangerous. We need to be prepared for anything."

That Evening

Later, Maya sat by herself in a quiet corner of the safe house, reflecting on everything that had happened. She had given everything to tell Lily's story and expose the network, but now she was beginning to wonder what it would take to truly end this.

Suddenly, her phone buzzed again. This time, it was an encrypted message from a contact she hadn't heard from in years: an investigative journalist named Tom Rivera. Tom had been a mentor to her early in her career and was known for his hard-hitting stories on government corruption.

The message was short but urgent:

"Meet me at the old coffee shop. Midnight. I have information that will help you finish this."

Maya's heart skipped a beat. She hadn't spoken to Tom since he'd disappeared from the journalism scene after a major story went cold. She quickly told The Archivist and Jules about the message.

"It could be a trap," The Archivist warned, his brow furrowed. "They could have intercepted your old contacts and are using them against you."

Maya considered this, but something told her that Tom wouldn't betray her, especially not now. "It's worth the risk. If there's a chance, he has information that could bring down the network completely, we have to take it."

Jules and The Archivist exchanged a glance, and then Jules nodded. "We'll be close by. If anything happens, we'll get you out of there."

At Midnight

Maya arrived at the dimly lit coffee shop where she'd agreed to meet Tom. The place was almost deserted, with only a barista wiping down tables and a couple huddling in a corner. She took a seat at the back, her nerves on edge as she waited. She could see her reflection in the window, her face hardened and determined, the face of someone who had come too far to turn back.

Moments later, a man in a worn jacket and a baseball cap walked in, his face partially obscured. Maya immediately recognized him—Tom Rivera. He approached her table, nodding in greeting as he sat down across from her.

"Maya," he said quietly, his eyes scanning the room. "You've stirred up quite the storm."

"Wasn't that always the plan?" she replied with a smirk, though her voice betrayed her exhaustion.

Tom leaned in, lowering his voice. "Listen, I'm here because I still have connections—people in places you wouldn't believe. They've been watching your story, and some of them are willing to talk. They're ready to give you what you need to finish this."

Maya's heart raced. "Why now?"

"Because you've broken their shield," he replied. "They thought they were untouchable, and now they're running scared. But you need to be careful, Maya. They're not going to go down without a fight, and the people at the very top... they're worse than anything you've faced so far."

She nodded, absorbing his words. "What do you have for me?"

Tom got into his jacket and pulled out a small notebook, handing it to her. "Inside are names, locations, records of off-the-books meetings—all tied to the core of the network. It's the last piece of the puzzle. If you can corroborate this, it'll be enough to bring them down completely."

Maya took the notebook, feeling the weight of it in her hands. This was the final evidence she needed to finish what she'd started.

"Thank you, Tom," she said, her voice thick with gratitude. "You have no idea how much this means."

He smiled, a hint of pride in his expression. "You're doing good work, Maya. Be careful."

Back at the safe house, Maya, The Archivist, and Jules pored over the notebook, cross-referring the names and locations with the information they'd already gathered. With every page, they unraveled more of the network's structure, their hidden assets, and their influence over powerful institutions. They had everything they needed to expose the core of the organization and the leaders who had evaded accountability for so long.

They worked tirelessly, compiling the final report, double-checking every fact, every connection. The morning sun was just starting to rise as they finished, exhaustion settling over them like a blanket. But it was a victorious exhaustion—they had done it. They had everything.

Just as they prepared to release the final report, there was a loud bang on the door. Maya froze, her heart racing as she glanced at The Archivist and Jules. They all knew what this could mean.

Jules quickly checked the security cameras. "It's them," she whispered, her face pale. "They've found us."

Without hesitation, The Archivist grabbed the laptop with the report. "Get to the back door," he said urgently. "I'll create a diversion. You two get out of here and get this report online."

"No!" Maya protested, her voice breaking. "We can't just leave you."

The Archivist gave her a sad smile. "This is my fight too, Maya. I've spent years trying to bring them down. If this is the cost, then so be it."

Jules tugged on her arm, urgency in her eyes. "Maya, we must go. If we lose this report, everything we've done will be for nothing."

Reluctantly, Maya followed Jules, glancing back one last time as The Archivist moved toward the front of the safe house. She and Jules slipped out the back, running into dawn as they heard the struggle behind them.

They didn't stop running until they reached a secure location, a small storage unit where they'd hidden backup drives of the final report. Jules quickly plugged in the drive, uploading the files to every outlet and platform they had on standby.

As they watched the upload complete, Maya felt a bittersweet sense of relief. They had done it. The world would see the truth, and the network would finally fall.

But as she looked at Jules, she knew they had both paid a heavy price. The Archivist's sacrifice weighed heavily on her, a reminder of the cost of justice. Yet she knew that he had given them the chance to finish what he had started years ago.

They sat together in silence as the report spread across the world, knowing that they had taken down something far bigger than themselves. And as the news of the network's collapse flooded their screens, Maya knew that Lily's story—and the stories of all those who had been silenced—had finally been heard.

But even as they celebrated, Maya couldn't shake the feeling that this victory was only the beginning. The truth had come to light, but the shadows they had uncovered ran deep, and she knew there would be more battles to fight.

For now, though, she allowed herself a moment of quiet satisfaction. She had faced the darkness—and won.

13

Aftermath and Reckoning

The following days were a whirlwind of reactions, fallout, and relief. The exposé of the network's leaders spread globally, igniting demands for investigations, resignations, and justice. Public outcry grew louder with each passing hour, and several members of the network, including key political figures and business moguls, were arrested or questioned. News anchors struggled to keep up with the constant updates as the world watched the powerful elite fall one by one.

But for Maya, the triumph felt hollow. She and Jules had lost The Archivist, a mentor and friend who had dedicated his life to the truth. The cost of their victory weighed heavily on her, and she struggled to balance her sense of accomplishment with the lingering pain of loss. She knew he would be proud of what they had achieved, yet his absence left a gap that she couldn't fill.

Maya stayed hidden during the first few days after the release, watching the events unfold from the safety of Jules's apartment. The two women shared a quiet bond, their grief unspoken but understood. Both of them knew that, despite their success, there would be lingering danger. The network's remaining members, though weakened, would be searching for revenge, and Maya was still a prime target.

A Week LaterOn the seventh day after the final release, Maya received a message from the police. They had identified The Archivist's body at the safe house and wanted to question her as the last known associate. Maya's stomach twisted at the thought of recounting those final moments, but she agreed to meet with them. She knew that part of honoring The Archivist's sacrifice was ensuring that the full story was told, even the painful parts.

She arrived at the police station early the next morning, her mind filled with memories of her journey—of Lily, The Archivist, the warehouse, and all the moments that had led her here. She was greeted by Detective Harris, a stern yet sympathetic man who had been following the case closely.

"Miss Patel," he said, extending a hand. "Thank you for coming in. I know this isn't easy."

Maya nodded, her voice steady despite the turmoil within her. "I'm here to make sure you understand what happened. The Archivist deserves that much."

The detective led her into an interview room, where she recounted the story from the beginning: her discovery of Lily's body, her investigation into the Rogue Guardians, her journey with The Archivist and Jules, and the final confrontation at the safe house. As she spoke, she realized the enormity of what they had accomplished, but also the weight of what they had sacrificed.

When she finished, Detective Harris leaned forward, his gaze intense. "Miss Patel, I want you to know that your work has set off a series of high-level investigations. You and your team have exposed corruption at every level, and it's clear you're going to be remembered as one of the most courageous whistleblowers in recent history."

Maya's chest tightened, her gratitude mingling with sorrow. "I didn't do it alone. I had people who believed in me, people who... who gave their lives for this."

The detective nodded, his expression softening. "I understand. And rest assured, we'll make sure the world knows about The Archivist's role in this. He won't be forgotten."

Two Weeks Later

Life didn't return to normal for Maya. She was in high demand, her inbox filled with interview requests, book deals, and messages from people inspired by her story. Despite the risks, she chose to reappear publicly, knowing that her visibility offered a layer of protection from the network's remaining members. If she hid, they might think they'd won. But if she continued to speak out, they'd know she wasn't afraid.

One morning, while checking her messages, she found an unexpected email from a familiar address. It was from Richard, the former Rogue Guardian who had first warned her about the network's true scope. His message was brief but loaded with implications:

"They're still out there, regrouping. The network has deeper roots than you know. Be vigilant. You've cut off one branch, but the tree remains."

Maya's blood ran cold. She had suspected that the power structure was too vast, too entrenched to be destroyed. She knew that remnants of the network would regroup, perhaps under a new name or new leadership. She forwarded the message to Jules, her mind already working through their next steps.

Later That Day

Maya met Jules at a quiet coffee shop, where they discussed Richard's email and their options going forward. The two women had become a formidable team, and despite the risks, both felt compelled to continue the fight.

"We knew this wasn't going to be a one-time battle," Jules said, her voice steady but resolute. "We took down a significant part of the network, but as long as there are people willing to exploit power, there will be new threats."

Maya nodded, her gaze distant. "We've inspired people, though. We've shown that the truth can't stay buried forever. And if we can keep that momentum going, we can fight back."

Jules smiled, a glint of defiance in her eyes. "Then let's do it. Let's build something new—an organization that holds the powerful accountable. We can work with other whistleblowers, investigative journalists, anyone who wants to expose corruption."

The idea was bold, but it resonated with Maya. They could create a coalition, a network of truth-seekers who would continue to uncover the secrets that those in power tried to keep hidden. It would be dangerous work, but the rewards were worth the risk.

And so, they made a pact. They would dedicate themselves to this mission, using their skills and connections to keep exposing the hidden corruption that plagued the world.

The First Case

A month later, Maya and Jules launched their new organization, The Vigilant. They operated quietly, partnering with trusted journalists and former activists who had once been silenced by the network.

Their first major case focused on a corporation linked to environmental destruction and worker exploitation, one that had managed to evade legal consequences for years. With Maya's experience and Jules's knowledge of the network's tactics, they began gathering evidence, working from the shadows to protect their sources.

They released their first report under The Vigilant banner, and it quickly gained traction. People were beginning to recognize their symbol and mission, and slowly, more whistleblowers and allies came forward, eager to join the fight.

Maya felt a renewed sense of purpose. She still thought of Lily often, of the girl who had sparked this journey and who had given her life for the truth. Every story they exposed, every injustice they brought to light, was a tribute to Lily's memory.

One Year Later

A year after the fall of the Rogue Guardians, Maya and Jules established The Vigilant as a respected, if mysterious, organization. They had faced threats, opposition, and even attempts to silence them, but their work continued. They had grown, expanding their team, building connections, and establishing a network of informants who trusted them to protect their identities.

One afternoon, Maya received a package with no return address. She opened it cautiously, finding a single envelope inside. It contained a letter, handwritten, in a familiar scrawl.

"Maya,

I told you before—there's more to this than you'll ever know. You've done well, but don't let your guard down. Power has a way of surviving, of finding new faces and new names. Keep fighting, and remember that for every truth uncovered, a hundred more lie waiting in the dark."

—Richard

Maya closed the letter, a sense of both determination and caution settling over her. Richard's words were a reminder of the path she had chosen, a path that would be fraught with challenges. But she was no longer afraid of the darkness. She had faced it, exposed it, and emerged stronger than she ever thought possible.

As she looked around her small office, her gaze rested on a framed photograph of Lily, a quiet reminder of why she had started this journey. She had fought for the truth, for justice, and for countless others who might one day follow her lead.

And if she had a voice, she would continue to fight. For Lily. For The Archivist. For every person who had been silenced.

Because now, the shadows held no power over her.

14

The Echoes of Power

Months had passed since Maya received Richard's letter, but his words lingered in her mind. Power has a way of surviving. She understood now that even as The Vigilant fought to expose the darkness, there would always be new shadows to uncover. But the growth of The Vigilant had given her hope—each new ally, each whistleblower, each witness to injustice strengthened their mission and gave Maya a sense of purpose that extended far beyond her initial journey with Lily.

The organization has now expanded internationally, with dedicated teams stationed in key cities around the world. They were no longer just Maya and Jules; they were a network of truth-seekers, dedicated to dismantling systems of corruption and oppression wherever they found them. But as The Vigilant grew, so did the threats against it.

The Call for Help

One late evening, as Maya prepared to leave her office, she received a message from a contact in Paris. It was from a journalist named Camille Dupont, who had been investigating a financial institution tied to human trafficking and money laundering. Camille's message was terse and urgent:

"They know I'm onto them. Need help. Information compromised. Can I trust The Vigilant?"

Maya's heart skipped a beat. She'd heard about Camille's work—a series of articles that had rocked the Parisian elite and exposed corporate scandals that had gone unnoticed for years. But this was different; Camille was dealing with a powerful international syndicate, one that was ruthless and well-connected.

She forwarded the message to Jules, who replied almost immediately.

"This could be huge, Maya. But we must be careful. If Camille's been exposed, we need to get her out before it's too late."

Maya agreed. They couldn't let a journalist fighting for justice face such danger alone. The Vigilant had resources in Europe now, including safe houses, allies in law enforcement, and a network of trusted contacts who could help protect Camille. It was risky, but they needed to move fast.

The Mission in Paris

Maya and Jules flew to Paris within 24 hours, coordinating with their European team to prepare a safe extraction plan for Camille. Their Paris contact, a former intelligence officer named Henri, met them upon arrival. Henri was an old friend of The Archivist's, and he had become an asset to The Vigilant, providing critical intelligence and logistical support.

Henri greeted them with a grim expression. "Camille's in more trouble than we thought," he said as he led them to a secure location. "The syndicate she's investigating has connections across Europe. They've already sent people after her twice."

Maya felt a surge of anger. She knew that Camille's story could expose a vast network of illegal activities that had been shielded by wealth and power. But getting her out safely would require precision and courage.

They devised a plan to meet Camille at a quiet café near the Seine. Maya and Jules would approach first, with Henri's team positioned nearby for backup. Camille would have to leave Paris quickly and go hiding until The Vigilant could find a secure location for her.

The Meeting with Camille

The café was quiet, the late afternoon sun casting long shadows across Cobblestone Street. Maya and Jules took a table near the back, scanning the room as they waited. Moments later, Camille entered, her eyes darting around nervously. She was young, in her late twenties, with an air of defiance tempered by the weariness of someone who had seen too much.

Camille took a seat across from them, her voice a whisper. "Thank you for coming. I didn't know who else to trust."

Maya leaned in, her gaze steady. "You're not alone, Camille. The Vigilant has resources. We can protect you, but you must be honest with us. How much do they know?"

Camille took a shaky breath. "They know I have evidence—documents, wire transfers, names of high-profile clients. I've been getting threats for weeks, but last night they sent someone to my apartment. They want me to back off, to disappear."

Maya exchanged a glance with Jules, then reached for Camille's hand. "We're going to get you out of here. But you must trust us and follow our instructions exactly.

Camille nodded, her face, a mixture of relief and fear. "I don't know how they found out, but they have contacts everywhere. Even the police aren't safe."

Jules spoke calmly, her voice soothing. "That's why we're here. We have contacts of our own, people who owe us favors. Once we get you to the safe house, we'll extract the information you have and expose everything."

Camille's eyes filled with determination. "I'm ready. They won't silence me."

The Escape

As they left the café, Henri's team shadowed them at a distance, watching for any signs of trouble. They led Camille down narrow alleyways and through side streets, avoiding main roads to evade surveillance. Paris at dusk was beautiful, but Maya could only focus on the mission, her nerves taut as they navigated the city.

Just as they neared the safe house, a black car screeched to a stop at the corner, and two men in suits stepped out, their eyes scanning the area. Henri's voice crackled over the radio. "We have hostiles. Take the alternate route."

Maya took Camille's hand, pulling her into a nearby alley as Jules covered their rear. They moved quickly, ducking through narrow passageways and weaving through crowds until they reached a secondary safe house hidden within an old bookstore. Once inside, Henri's team secured the entrances, and everyone took a breath.

Camille looked at Maya, her expression resolute despite the fear in her eyes. "I'll give you everything I have. It's all on my laptop, encrypted and hidden. If we can get it to a secure network, you'll have enough to take them down."

Jules nodded. "We'll extract the data tonight and send it to our trusted contacts in the media. This will go live by morning."

The Evidence Unveiled

That night, with Camille's information in hand, Maya and Jules worked tirelessly to decode and verify the documents. The files painted a damning picture: a sophisticated money-laundering operation that funneled millions through various shell companies across Europe, all under the guise of legitimate businesses. The syndicate was connected to major banks, politicians, and even entertainment figures. They had created a seemingly impenetrable empire, one that had profited from exploitation and corruption for years.

By dawn, the files were ready. Maya sent the data to trusted journalists across Europe, ensuring that the story would be told by those who could amplify its reach. With The Vigilant's protection, Camille would be safe, at least for now.

The Response

The reaction was immediate. News outlets picked up the story, and soon, headlines around the world were exposing the syndicate's crimes. Politicians scrambled to issue statements distancing themselves from the accused, while banks involved in the scheme faced an intense public backlash. Camille's story became a rallying cry, a symbol of resilience against powerful forces that had tried to silence her.

As the world took notice, Maya and Jules received messages of support from allies around the globe. The Vigilant had struck again, delivering a powerful blow to a corrupt network and sending a clear message: No matter how powerful, no one was above accountability.

But as the days passed, Maya received another anonymous message, reminding her of the ever-present danger:

"Well done, Maya. But you're only touching the surface. This goes deeper than you can imagine. If you continue, be prepared for a war."

The words were chilling, but Maya read them with calm resolve. She had seen the worst of humanity, and she knew there would always be forces trying to pull her back. But she also knew she wasn't alone. She had built a network of allies, people like Camille, Jules, and Henri, who believed in the power of truth and justice.

The shadows might always be there, but now, Maya and The Vigilant were the light exposing them. And she would continue fighting, knowing that for every corrupt network they dismantled, countless lives would be saved, countless truths would be heard, and the world would inch closer to justice.

Maya closed her laptop and looked out at the Paris skyline, feeling a sense of fulfillment she hadn't felt in years. She had chosen a path fraught with danger, but it was a path she could no longer abandon. For Lily, for The Archivist, for Camille, and for everyone who had been silenced, she would keep fighting.

Because some battles were worth every risk, every sacrifice, and every step into the darkness.

And as she watched the sunrise over Paris, Maya knew she was ready for whatever came next.

15

New Frontlines

Two weeks after the Paris operation, The Vigilant had become a symbol of resilience. People everywhere began reaching out, emboldened by Camille's story and inspired by the organization's courage. The ripple effect was palpable whistleblowers from all corners of the world sent messages, desperate to expose injustices within their industries, governments, and communities.

But while the public embraced The Vigilant, powerful enemies loomed closer than ever. Threats became more frequent and more direct, a reminder that the forces Maya and her team were up against would stop at nothing to protect their empires.

A New Message

One evening, as Maya sifted through her overflowing inbox, a message from Richard arrived. His emails had become sporadic, each one brief and cryptic, offering glimpses into the deeper network they had only begun to uncover. This message, however, was different. It was longer, filled with urgency and a stark warning:

"Maya, they're regrouping under a new name. The survivors of your last exposé are collaborating with a syndicate from Eastern Europe—a group far more ruthless, with ties to arms dealing, drug trafficking, and even the intelligence community. They call themselves The Consortium. You need to be cautious. If you pursue this, you'll be confronting power on an unprecedented scale."

Maya sat back, feeling the weight of his words. The Consortium. This new threat felt even more dangerous than the network she had dismantled. She knew that to take them on, The Vigilant would need allies and resources far beyond what they had ever needed before.

She immediately forwarded the message to Jules, who called her within minutes.

"This is big, Maya," Jules said, her voice tense. "We've faced dangerous people before, but nothing like this. If Richard's right, we're talking about an organization with the power to destabilize entire regions."

Maya took a deep breath, her mind already racing with ideas. "Then we need to prepare. We can't go into this blind. Let's gather every resource we have—contacts, allies, former intelligence assets. If we're going to fight The Consortium, we need to be stronger than ever."

Rallying the Allies

Over the following days, Maya and Jules began reaching out to their network, piecing together a coalition of allies from around the world. Among them was Henri in Paris, along with former journalists, whistleblowers, and security experts who had assisted The Vigilant in the past. They knew this operation would require precision, strategy, and unwavering commitment. But they also knew that, with the right people, they could confront even the most dangerous of adversaries.

As they prepared, Maya received an encrypted call from a woman identifying herself only as "Raven." She was a former intelligence operative with expertise in Eastern European syndicates, and she claimed to have vital information about The Consortium's structure.

"You're up against more than just a criminal network," Raven warned, her voice calm but intense. "The Consortium has ties to governments, private militaries, and deep-rooted alliances. If you try to bring them down, they'll come to you with everything they have.

Maya felt a chill but remained resolute. "We're ready to face them. But if you have information, we could use it. We're gathering a team."

There was a pause before Raven replied, her tone softening. "I'll help. But understand this: once you're in, there's no turning back. The Consortium doesn't forgive or forget."

Maya accepted her help, knowing this alliance could be a game-changer. With Raven's intelligence and the coalition, they had formed, they could go after The Consortium with the precision of a military operation.

First Strike

With Raven's intel and Henri's support, The Vigilant launched its first investigation into The Consortium's dealings. They identified a shell corporation in Dubai, one that funneled funds through offshore accounts to finance illegal arms trades across Eastern Europe. This was their starting point, and Maya's team began tracking each transaction, following the money trail back to The Consortium's leaders.

But every new discovery brought fresh danger. One night, as Maya reviewed the latest financial documents, a notification appeared on her screen. Someone was attempting to breach The Vigilant's secure server. She immediately alerted Jules, who ran to her side.

"It's them," Jules said, her eyes wide with concern. "They're trying to shut us down before we even get started."

Maya quickly activated the countermeasures she'd installed after the Rogue Guardians' attack, rerouting the server through multiple layers of encryption. She watched as the attempted breach was blocked, but she knew this was only the beginning.

"They're testing our defenses," Maya muttered. "They're seeing how far we'll go—and how well we're prepared."

Jules nodded; her gaze resolute. "Let's show them we're ready."

A Deadly Encounter

As their investigation intensified, Maya and Raven uncovered The Consortium's next move: a high-profile gala in London, where its leaders would meet to finalize deals with wealthy financiers. It was the perfect opportunity to intercept them, to gather firsthand evidence of their influence and connections.

Maya and Jules flew to London with Henri, coordinating with local allies to arrange covert surveillance at the event. They knew they had one shot to document the meeting, and the risks were high. If The Consortium identified them, there would be immediate consequences.

At the gala, Maya posed as a journalist covering the charity aspect of the event, blending in with the crowd as she captured footage of the attendees. She spotted several known criminals, politicians, and business elites mingling as if they were old friends. The wealth and influence in the room were a staggering reminder of just how formidable The Consortium's reach was.

As she made her way through the event, Maya noticed a familiar face: Richard. He was there, mingling with high-ranking members of The Consortium, his calm but watchful demeanor. Their eyes met briefly, and he gave her the faintest nod, an acknowledgment of their shared understanding.

But just as Maya began recording him, a security guard approached, his gaze fixed on her with suspicion.

"Excuse me, ma'am. Can I see your press credentials?" he asked, his voice firm.

Maya felt her heart race. She knew her cover was thin, and one wrong move could blow the entire operation.

Thinking quickly, she smiled, pulling out a fabricated press ID she had created for this very scenario. "Of course. I'm with Global Review—just covering the charitable side of the event."

The guard glanced at her badge, then at her camera, before finally nodding. "Very well but stay in the designated press area."

Maya exhaled, relieved, and quickly returned to her surveillance. She spotted Raven across the room, capturing footage of two men negotiating in hushed voices near the bar. Everything was going according to plan, but she knew they had to act fast before their cover was blown.

Escape and Revelation

As the night wound down, Maya and her team gathered in a secluded area to compare their findings. They had captured valuable footage of Consortium members, conversations hinting at illegal deals, and incriminating exchanges with politicians. It was enough to launch a massive exposé.

But just as they prepared to leave, an alarm blared through the venue. Security personnel began sealing exits, and Maya realized with a sinking feeling that The Consortium had discovered their presence.

"We need to get out, now," Raven whispered urgently. "They'll have eyes on every exit."

The team moved quickly, blending into the crowd as they navigated through service hallways and emergency exits. Maya felt adrenaline surge through her veins as they sprinted down a narrow corridor, trying to stay ahead of the guards pursuing them.

In a stroke of luck, Henri had arranged a car outside the venue, and they piled into it, breathless but exhilarated. As they sped away from the gala, Maya glanced at her camera, knowing they had obtained invaluable evidence.

Once they were safely back at their temporary headquarters, they reviewed the footage. Every frame, every voice, every handshake—they had documented a web of corruption that tied The Consortium to some of the most powerful individuals across Europe.

The Next Phase

With the footage and information compiled, Maya and The Vigilant prepared for the release of their findings. They knew this report would be their most dangerous yet, one that would provoke powerful enemies and potentially put lives at risk. But it was a necessary step in their mission to bring The Consortium to justice.

The release was scheduled for the following day, a carefully coordinated operation involving media outlets, journalists, and political contacts across multiple countries. Maya stayed up late that night, reflecting on everything they had uncovered and the risks they were about to take.

Jules joined her, placing a reassuring hand on her shoulder. "This is bigger than anything we've ever done, Maya. But we're ready."

Maya nodded, a fierce determination in her eyes. "For Lily, for The Archivist, and for everyone who has been silenced—we're ready."

The Morning of the Release

The morning arrived with a sense of calm that belied the storm about to unfold. At precisely 9:00 AM, The Vigilant's findings went live, accompanied by a flood of news reports from their media allies. Within minutes, The Consortium's name was trending worldwide, the shocking evidence drawing intense scrutiny from governments, activists, and the public.

The backlash was immediate. Protests erupted across Europe, calling for justice and accountability, and politicians scrambled to denounce their connections to the syndicate. The Consortium's leaders went hiding, their assets frozen, their influence shattered.

Maya felt bittersweet satisfaction as she watched the world's response. They had struck a powerful blow, but she knew The Consortium would regroup, rebranding itself, finding new ways to protect its interests.

Still, The Vigilant had proven its strength, and the world was watching. They had become a force that even the most powerful syndicates could not ignore. And as Maya looked around at her team, she knew they were ready to face whatever came next.

Because the fight for justice never ended—it only transformed. And Maya, Jules, and The Vigilant were prepared to stand on the frontlines, exposing darkness wherever it hid, with the memory of those they had lost guiding them forward.

16

Under Siege

The exposé on The Consortium sent shockwaves through global media, sparking investigations, resignations, and mounting pressure on governments to crack down on corruption. For Maya and The Vigilant, the release was a hard-won victory, a testament to the power of truth against unimaginable odds. But it also brought an unsettling awareness: they were now targets on a scale they had never experienced.

In the days following the report, Maya kept a low profile. She and Jules knew that The Consortium's remaining members would seek revenge, and they were ready for retaliatory strikes. They'd upgraded The Vigilant's security systems and moved their headquarters to an undisclosed location, but they couldn't shake the feeling that The Consortium was closer than ever.

A New Threat Emerges

Late one night, as Maya reviewed encrypted messages on her laptop, an unfamiliar code sequence appeared on the screen. She recognized it immediately—a signature she'd seen only once before. The Consortium's top hacker, known only as "Sable." His skills were legendary, and he'd managed to breach systems that were thought to be impenetrable.

Maya's screen flickered, and then a message appeared:

"I warned you not to interfere, Maya. Consider this your last chance to walk away."

Before she could react, her laptop froze, and every document on the screen vanished, replaced by a black screen bearing The Consortium's symbol: a single eye, veiled in shadows. A chill ran through her, but she quickly rebooted, activating backup protocols she and Jules had designed for emergencies. Within minutes, she'd regained access to most of the files, but she knew Sable's message was clear: The Consortium was watching, and they were coming.

She alerted Jules, who immediately sprang into action, mobilizing The Vigilant's cyber defense team and setting up temporary headquarters to avoid further tracking. They doubled their efforts to secure every piece of data, every communication, and every connection to their allies.

The Attack on Headquarters

Days later, while Maya and her team continued reinforcing their defenses, an even more sinister attack arrived—this time in person. A group of armed intruders broke into The Vigilant's headquarters, setting off security alarms and forcing the team to take immediate action.

Maya and Jules led the team to a fortified safe room, where they monitored the security cameras. The attackers moved methodically, disabling security systems, their faces hidden behind masks.

Jules clenched her fists, her voice tense. "They're professionals. The Consortium sent them to wipe us out."

Maya nodded, adrenaline surging through her. "We've prepared for this. Let's keep everyone calm and focus on getting our most critical data out."

With quick thinking, they transferred sensitive files to encrypted drives and uploaded backups to offsite servers, ensuring that The Vigilant's work would survive even if the headquarters fell. Then, Maya sent an emergency alert to trusted allies, signaling their need for backup.

The attackers reached the safe room door, pounding against it. The Vigilant team held their ground, but every second felt like a countdown to something catastrophic. Just as Maya began to wonder if help would arrive in time, a voice came through her earpiece.

"It's Henri. We're five minutes out. Hold tight."

Relief flooded through her. Henri's team arrived moments later, expertly neutralizing the attackers and securing the building. When the dust settled, Maya and her team emerged from the safe room, shaken but unbroken.

Henri approached her, a grim expression on his face. "This was just the beginning, Maya. The Consortium's making a statement—they're not going down without a fight."

A Strategic Retreat

Realizing the danger of remaining in one location, The Vigilant temporarily disbanded, with each team member relocating to different parts of the world. Maya and Jules traveled to South America, where they could operate under the radar and continue investigating The Consortium's inner circle from a safe distance.

In their remote hideout, Maya and Jules reached out to their global allies, gathering intel and coordinating efforts. They knew they'd need more than just information this time—they needed allies with influence and the means to counter The Consortium's reach.

Raven, their intelligent contact, remained a steadfast partner. She helped Maya and Jules connect with international figures—human rights advocates, financial experts, and former diplomats—each of whom had their own reasons to oppose The Consortium. Their new coalition began to take shape, a patchwork of courageous individuals from all walks of life.

One contact, a former finance minister from Eastern Europe named Dmitri, provided invaluable insights into The Consortium's financial operations. "Their funds are hidden in accounts across multiple countries," he explained. "They use shell companies to move money through the international system. But if you can track the funds to their core accounts, you can cut off their resources."

With Dmitri's help, The Vigilant began tracing the money trail. The Consortium's vast financial network started to come into focus, and Maya knew they were getting closer to a way to destabilize it from within.

A Return to Richard

During their efforts, Maya received another encrypted message from Richard, this time with an urgent request to meet. He was in Vienna and claimed to have critical information on The Consortium's leadership.

Maya and Jules debated the risks but ultimately decided to go. Richard had been a valuable source, and they needed every edge they could get. Traveling under aliases, they arrived in Vienna and met Richard in a discreet café.

Richard looked more worn than the last time Maya had seen him, his eyes filled with a wary determination. "I'm taking a risk coming here," he said. "But you need to know something. The Consortium isn't just a network of criminals and corrupt officials. They're connected to a secret faction within the intelligence community—people who use the organization for covert operations and black-market deals."

Maya felt her stomach drop. "You're saying The Consortium has government protection?"

Richard nodded. "Not officially, of course. But certain factions have been using them for years, treating them as assets to accomplish what can't be done through official channels. If you expose these connections, it could bring down their entire support structure—but it will also put you in the crosshairs of people even more dangerous than The Consortium."

Jules leaned forward; her voice was fierce. "If we do this, it must be airtight. No room for doubt, no gaps in the story."

Richard slid a USB drive across the table. "This has everything I've gathered—names, locations, encrypted messages. But be careful. If they realize what you're planning, they'll use every resource they must stop you."

Maya took the drive, her determination stronger than her fear. "We'll take that risk. It's time The Consortium's true nature is exposed."

A Daring Plan

Back in their South American hideout, Maya and Jules analyzed Richard's files. The data revealed a disturbing pattern of covert operations involving high-ranking officials, clandestine arms deals, and espionage missions. They quickly understood the gravity of their task. This wasn't just about exposing The Consortium anymore; it was about uncovering a shadow government that used the organization as a puppet.

Maya contacted their allies in journalism and human rights, arranging for a coordinated release of the findings. They knew this would be their most dangerous exposé yet, one that would likely lead to severe consequences. But there was no turning back now.

They decided on a multi-pronged approach, timing the release of information across several international platforms to ensure that the data couldn't be suppressed. Maya, Jules, and their coalition of allies worked tirelessly, preparing for the release.

The Final Countdown

As the release date approached, Maya and Jules took extra precautions, setting up fail-safes to protect the information and their identities. They knew the moment the report went live, they'd be putting themselves in grave danger. But they also knew the truth needed to be told.

The night before the release, Maya and Jules shared a quiet moment, reflecting on their journey. They had come so far, faced unthinkable challenges, and lost people they cared about along the way. But through it all, they had remained unbreakable.

"This could change everything, Maya," Jules said, a mixture of pride and apprehension in her voice. "After tomorrow, there's no going back."

Maya nodded; a calm determination settled over her. "We're doing this for all the people who couldn't. For Lily, for The Archivist, for everyone who's been silenced."

Jules smiled, reaching for her hand. "Then let's make sure it counts."

The Release

The next morning, the exposé went live. The world watched as The Vigilant's findings spread, implicating some of the most powerful figures in a conspiracy that spanned borders and industries. The backlash was immediate. Protests erupted in major cities, demanding accountability, transparency, and an end to the hidden influence of The Consortium.

But even as the story dominated headlines, Maya and Jules knew they had to stay vigilant. They had struck a blow, but they could feel the weight of an impending retaliation.

Later that evening, Maya received a final message from Richard:

"They know it was you, Maya. They'll come for you but remember—you're not alone. The world is on your side now."

Maya smiled to herself, feeling both the gravity and the triumph of their actions. They had fought the darkness and won, shining a light on the shadows that had long controlled the world.

But even as she prepared to face whatever came next, she felt a profound sense of peace. The Vigilant had shown the world that the truth could not be silenced, that justice could prevail, and that courage was more powerful than fear.

As night fell, Maya knew the fight was far from over. But for the first time, she felt certain that the truth would endure—and that if she had allies like Jules, Richard, and the countless people standing with The Vigilant, they would continue to expose the darkness, one battle at a time.

17

A World Awakens

The fallout from The Vigilant's exposé continued to reverberate across the globe. Politicians and CEOs were arrested, resignations flooded the headlines, and investigations into The Consortium reached the highest levels of government. But for Maya and her team, the battle was far from over.

In the days following the release, The Vigilant became both a beacon of hope and a lightning rod for threats. Supporters rallied to their cause, hailing them as heroes, while those connected to The Consortium seethed with anger, launching a coordinated smear campaign to discredit Maya, Jules, and their allies.

To counter these attacks, Maya knew they had to stay active, visible, and ahead of their enemies. As public interest surged, Maya and Jules focused on strengthening The Vigilant, not only to withstand the backlash but to build something that would last—a network that could continue the fight for truth, no matter the cost.

Reinforcements Arrive

One evening, as Maya and Jules were strategizing their next steps, Raven sent an encrypted message with urgent news.

"I've found allies within the intelligence community. Former agents, analysts, people who've seen the dark side of The Consortium and want it to be gone. They're willing to join us, but they'll need assurances of anonymity."

Maya felt a spark of hope. This was exactly what they needed—insiders who understood The Consortium's methods, people who could protect The Vigilant from within the shadows.

She messaged Raven back, setting up a secure line for communication. The next day, Raven introduced them to the first few allies: a cyber intelligence expert, a former counterintelligence operative, and a whistleblower who had previously worked with The Consortium. Each of them had their own reasons for joining, each with a story of betrayal, fear, and, ultimately, courage.

With these new resources, The Vigilant expanded its defenses, implementing state-of-the-art security measures and improving their encryption systems. They set up backup servers in undisclosed locations, ensuring their data would survive even if they were directly attacked again. Their team was no longer just a handful of idealists; they were becoming a sophisticated force for accountability.

The Threat Intensifies

Despite their precautions, the threats against The Vigilant escalated. A message arrived one night, slipped under the door of their safe house. It was written in an elegant script, and it read simply:

"You can't hide forever. Justice, like power, is controlled by those who can afford it. Remember that."

Maya felt a chill as she read the note, but her resolve only strengthened. She shared it with Jules, who looked at her, a fire in her eyes.

"They're afraid of us, Maya. That's why they're trying to scare us back into silence."

Maya nodded, folding the note carefully. "Then we don't back down. We dig deeper, we keep exposing them until there's nowhere left for them to hide."

The Consortium's Countermove

During the growing backlash, The Consortium made a drastic move. News outlets connected to their allies began releasing false stories about The Vigilant, accusing them of fabricating evidence, manipulating the public, and working as a front for political interests. The smears were sophisticated, each story carefully crafted to discredit everything Maya, and her team had achieved.

The impact was immediate. While many people continued to support The Vigilant, the accusations created doubt, especially among those unfamiliar with their work. Maya received messages from former allies and new supporters, asking for reassurance, seeking proof of her integrity.

Jules was the first to respond, organizing a live-streamed press conference to address the public. She spoke passionately, explaining the origins of The Vigilant, the risks they'd taken, and the sacrifices they'd made to bring justice to light.

"Our only agenda," she said, looking directly into the camera, "is the truth. We don't answer anyone but the people we fight for. And if we have breath in us, we'll continue to do just that."

The live broadcast went viral, reigniting support for The Vigilant and restoring faith in their mission. But Maya knew the battle wasn't over. They had fought back the tide, but The Consortium was still powerful, still lurking in the shadows.

The Alliance

After the broadcast, an unexpected ally reached out: an international human rights organization with connections in both governmental and non-governmental sectors. Their representative, a woman named Dr. Sofia Moreno, requested a private meeting with Maya and Jules to discuss a potential alliance.

Dr. Moreno had a reputation for fighting for justice in dangerous regions, and her organization was known for its effectiveness and fearlessness.

Maya and Jules met with her in a secure location, where Dr. Moreno got straight to the point.

"The Consortium has been a blight for years, Maya. We've watched them destabilize regions, exploit communities, and evade justice time and time again. If we join forces, we can amplify your message, protect your team, and ensure that the world doesn't forget the truth."

Maya listened, her heart pounding with hope. An alliance with Dr. Moreno's organization could mean a level of security and influence they'd never had before.

"What's the catch?" Jules asked, ever cautious.

Dr. Moreno smiled. "No catch. Just one condition: we operate in full transparency. No hidden agendas, no backroom deals. If we're in this, we're in it all the way."

Maya and Jules exchanged glances, both understanding the risks but also the potential. They agreed to the terms, sealing the alliance with a handshake. With Dr. Moreno's organization at their side, The Vigilant would have the strength to take their mission even further.

Uncovering The Consortium's Leaders

With renewed resources and an expanded network, The Vigilant set its sights on a new objective: identifying the leaders of The Consortium. Until now, these figures had operated behind layers of secrecy, using proxies and front companies to avoid exposure. But with the help of their new allies, Maya's team began dismantling these layers, slowly revealing the individuals behind the organization.

The investigation led them to a man named Viktor Malenko, a reclusive billionaire with extensive holdings in energy, tech, and arms manufacturing. Malenko was known for his philanthropy and his quiet influence in Eastern European politics, but the evidence suggested he was also one of The Consortium's primary financiers.

Maya's team gathered everything they could on Malenko—his business dealings, his political connections, his hidden investments. They connected the dots, tracking funds from Malenko's companies to Consortium-backed accounts and linking them to covert operations that had destabilized entire countries.

But Malenko wasn't acting alone. Their investigation revealed that he was part of a council of elites, each one responsible for a different aspect of The Consortium's operations. One controlled media influence, another managed logistics for arms deals, while another handled intelligence and security.

Unmasking these leaders would require strategy and caution, as each of them held immense power and influence. But Maya knew that taking down the core figures of The Consortium was the only way to dismantle the organization for good.

The Final Plan

Maya, Jules, and their allies formulated a plan to expose Malenko and the council. They coordinated with journalists, international law enforcement, and high-profile activists to ensure that the release would be global, reaching every corner of the world. This time, they wouldn't just tell the story—they would name names, linking each leader of The Consortium to documented crimes and human rights violations.

The release date was set. Maya felt a mixture of anticipation and dread, knowing that once this information went live, they would be placing themselves at the center of a storm like no other.

The night before the release, Maya received another message from Richard:

"Be careful, Maya. They know you're closing in. Some of them are already preparing to flee, but Malenko is doubling down. He's not going to let you expose him without a fight."

Maya replied with a simple, resolute message: "Let him try."

The Day of Reckoning

The exposé went live at dawn. The world watched as The Vigilant unveiled the truth behind Viktor Malenko and his council, exposing their corruption, their crimes, and their exploitation. The revelations were staggering, linking the council to atrocities that spanned decades, implicating them in war crimes, human trafficking, and financial manipulation.

The impact was immediate and overwhelming. Governments issued arrest warrants, companies cut ties with Malenko and his allies, and public protests erupted worldwide. The Vigilant had pulled the veil off a hidden empire, and the response was like nothing Maya had ever seen.

But as they celebrated their victory, they knew the danger had only intensified. Reports surfaced of Malenko fleeing his estate, his private jet departing in the dead of night. His associates, desperate to escape justice, scattered across the globe, hiding in fortified compounds, seeking refuge in countries without extradition.

Maya received one final message from Malenko himself, a chilling reminder of the battles yet to come:

"You may have won this round, Maya, but this war is far from over. Power is a force that never dies—it only changes form. You will always be hunted, always be in the shadows, because the truth is the most dangerous weapon of all.

She read the message with a steady gaze, unshaken. She had come to understand that the fight for truth was an endless one, a journey that would take everything she had. But she also knew that The Consortium's empire was crumbling, and she had a team of people as dedicated to justice as she was.

As she stood beside Jules, Raven, and her allies, watching the world respond to their work, Maya felt a profound sense of purpose. They had exposed one of the most dangerous organizations on the planet, and they would continue, even as new threats emerged from the shadows.

They would fight on, because for every secret they exposed, for every truth they revealed, the world became just a little brighter—and the forces of darkness just a little weaker.

18

The Battle Underground

The impact of The Vigilant's exposé on Viktor Malenko and The Consortium's leadership was undeniable. International law enforcement agencies mobilized like never before, launching investigations and seizing assets linked to The Consortium. Across the world, former allies of Malenko severed ties, desperate to distance themselves from the mounting scrutiny. But as The Vigilant celebrated its most significant victory to date, Maya and her team knew that The Consortium, or what remained of it, was far from finished.

In the weeks following the release, they went underground. The team scattered, setting up remote workstations and bunkers, relying on encrypted networks and trusted contacts. Maya knew that while the council was fractured, Malenko and his closest allies would be regrouping, planning their next move in the shadows.

A New Strategy

One evening, as Maya worked alone in her remote safe house, she received a call from Henri, her loyal ally in Paris.

"Are you sitting down?" he asked, his tone grave.

Maya felt a pang of worries. "What is it?"

"Interpol just released a new report. Malenko is rallying former Consortium operatives across Europe. They're forming splinter cells, targeting anyone who's been involved in the investigations, including journalists, activists, and former Consortium members who turned on him."

Maya clenched her fists, anger simmering within her. She knew this would happen; Malenko wouldn't accept defeat without a fight. "We knew he'd try to retaliate. But we can't let him regroup."

Henri agreed. "I've gathered intel on a few of these cells. If we strike quickly, we might be able to prevent them from gaining momentum. But we'll need to act fast."

Maya immediately contacted Jules and the rest of The Vigilant team, proposing a new operation. Instead of simply exposing The Consortium, they would actively disrupt its remnants, dismantling the splinter cells before they could fully reassemble.

Raven's Insight

To prepare for the operation, Maya contacted Raven, the former intelligence operative who had been a valuable ally in uncovering The Consortium's secrets. Raven had access to deep intelligence on criminal networks, and her connections were invaluable for this mission.

Raven listened as Maya laid out the plan, then responded with a mixture of caution and conviction. "You're about to engage with The Consortium's most dangerous elements. These are people who've been trained to operate in the shadows, and they're ruthless. But if we can cut off their resources, we'll leave them powerless."

Raven provided Maya with a detailed map of The Consortium's key safe houses, warehouses, and meeting points across Europe. Each location had been strategically chosen, hidden in plain sight within bustling cities or remote villages. The team split into smaller groups, each targeting a specific cell, ensuring that Malenko's remaining power would be chipped away piece by piece.

The First Strike

Maya's team first targeted a warehouse in Berlin, rumored to be a hub for arms trafficking and clandestine meetings. She led the team herself, accompanied by Jules, Henri, and two other trusted operatives from The Vigilant's European division. They had received intel that Malenko's associates were holding a meeting that evening, and they planned to intercept and capture any incriminating evidence left behind.

The warehouse was heavily guarded, with surveillance cameras and security teams patrolling the perimeter. Maya and her team moved carefully, blending into the shadows as they approached the building's side entrance. Jules disabled the cameras, and Henri signaled when it was clear to enter.

Inside, the warehouse was dimly lit, rows of crates lining the walls. They moved quietly, searching for any signs of the meeting. As they approached the back, voices echoed through the hall. Maya peered around the corner, spotting a small group of men gathered around a table, discussing plans in hushed tones.

She activated her recording device, capturing the conversation. The men spoke of retribution, of tracking down former allies who had turned against them, and of Malenko's orders to "restore control."

Jules signaled to move in, and the team quickly surrounded the group, catching them by surprise. Maya stepped forward, her voice firm. "It's over. We have enough evidence to ensure you'll never operate in this city again."

The men looked stunned, one of them reaching for a weapon, but Henri swiftly disarmed him. Within minutes, the operations were secured, and Maya's team began documenting everything in the warehouse: weapons caches, maps, documents. The entire operation took less than an hour, but they left with enough intel to dismantle Malenko's presence in Berlin.

Coordinated Strikes Across Europe

Over the next two weeks, The Vigilant conducted similar operations across Europe, taking down Consortium cells in Paris, Vienna, Madrid, and Rome. Each strike revealed more about Malenko's plans, exposing his desperate attempts to rebuild his network. But with every cell they dismantled, they weakened his control, stripping away his resources and limiting his reach.

In Rome, they uncovered a trove of documents that detailed financial transactions, linking Malenko's enterprises to hidden offshore accounts and shell corporations. This was a significant breakthrough—without his financial empire, Malenko would be unable to fund his operations or maintain his influence.

With the evidence in hand, The Vigilant collaborated with international authorities to freeze Malenko's assets, shutting down his remaining accounts and effectively bankrupting him. The once-powerful figure was now cornered, his empire was dismantled piece by piece.

The Final Confrontation

As Malenko's influence dwindled, his location was finally revealed through a tip from an anonymous source. He was hiding in a private estate in Montenegro, guarded by loyal operatives. The estate was heavily fortified, but The Vigilant knew that capturing Malenko was the final step in dismantling The Consortium once and for all.

Maya, Jules, and Raven assembled a team of elite operatives, coordinating with international authorities to approach the estate under the cover of night.

They moved through the thick forest surrounding the property, avoiding the guards as they approached the main house.

The atmosphere was tense, every sound amplified by the quiet of the night. They moved silently, their movements synchronized, each person in the team knowing the gravity of this moment. For many of them, this mission was not just about capturing Malenko—it was about justice for those who had suffered under his power.

They breached the estate with precision, moving through the hallways and securing each room as they advanced. Maya and Jules reached the main study, where they found Malenko, his face a mixture of anger and defiance.

"It's over, Malenko," Maya said, her voice steady. "You can't escape what you've done."

Malenko laughed, a bitter sound that echoed through the room. "You think you've won? I'm only one man. There will always be others to take my place. Power is a cycle, Maya. It never dies—it only changes hands."

Maya held his gaze, undeterred. "Maybe. But for today, you're finished. And every person you exploited, every life you destroyed—they'll finally see justice."

Raven and Jules secured Malenko as the rest of the team moved through the estate, collecting files, hard drives, and any remaining evidence. They knew that even with Malenko's arrest, there would be remnants of his network, hidden figures who would attempt to revive his empire. But for now, they had dealt a crippling blow to one of the most dangerous men in the world.

A New Dawn

The news of Malenko's capture spread rapidly, symbolizing a victory not just for The Vigilant, but for the global movement they had inspired. Across continents, people celebrated, feeling a renewed sense of hope. The story of The Vigilant became a rallying cry for justice, a testament to the power of courage and resilience in the face of corruption.

Back at their safe house, Maya and Jules finally allowed themselves a moment to breathe. They knew that their work was far from over, but this victory felt significant, a milestone in their journey.

Raven approached Maya, with a rare smile on her face. "You did it. Against all odds, you brought him down."

Maya nodded, her eyes reflecting a mixture of pride and determination. "We all did. And we'll keep fighting. Because if there are people like Malenko, there has to be someone willing to stand up to them."

Jules placed a hand on Maya's shoulder. "The Vigilant isn't just an organization anymore, Maya. It's a movement. And thanks to you, the world knows that justice isn't an impossible dream."

As dawn broke over the horizon, Maya looked out over the landscape, feeling a profound sense of purpose. They had fought for the truth, for those who had been silent, and for a world free from the grip of corrupt power.

But she knew that darkness would always linger, that the forces they'd fought would return in new forms, with new faces. And when they did, The Vigilant would be ready, standing as a beacon of justice, lighting the way for all who dared to seek the truth.

For Lily. For The Archivist. For everyone who fought before her and for those who would fight alongside her in the future. The mission was far from over, but Maya was no longer alone. Together, they were The Vigilant—and the world would never be the same.

19

Ripples in the Shadows

The capture of Viktor Malenko sent shockwaves through the underworld. As the news spread, many of his former allies either went hiding or attempted to strike new alliances, hoping to salvage what was left of their influence. For Maya, Jules, and the team at The Vigilant, Malenko's arrest was a turning point. Yet, even as the world celebrated, they remained vigilant, knowing that The Consortium's remnants would inevitably try to reassemble.

A Whisper of New Threats

One evening, Maya received a cryptic message on her private line. It was from an informant she'd met briefly during her investigations, a shadowy figure who went by the name "Echo." He was a former operative with ties to intelligence circles and had occasionally passed on information to The Vigilant when he felt it served his interests.

The message was brief:

"Malenko was only a pawn. Look for the one they call 'The Broker.' His reach is wider than you can imagine."

Maya felt a chill. She'd heard whispers of "The Broker" before—a name often mentioned in hushed conversations, rumored to control networks of crime syndicates, politicians, and corporations with the precision of a puppeteer. Unlike Malenko, The Broker remained invisible, a ghost who thrived in secrecy. If he truly was behind The Consortium, then Malenko's arrest had only scratched the surface.

She shared the message with Jules and the rest of the core team, including Raven, Henri, and Dr. Sofia Moreno. Each of them understood the significance of this new threat. They'd dismantled one part of the operation, but now they faced an even greater adversary, one with connections across borders, industries, and governments.

"We need to understand who The Broker really is," Raven said, her tone grave. "If Malenko was only a pawn, then this is bigger than we thought."

Henri nodded. "But how do we track down someone who's managed to stay invisible for so long? We'll need more than just informants. We need a way inside his circle."

Maya considered their options, a plan forming in her mind. "Then we find someone who knows his operations well. If he's been in the shadows this long, he's careful—but not invincible."

The Hunt for The Broker's Inner Circle

Over the next few weeks, The Vigilant set up an intricate operation, reaching out to former Consortium members who might know The Broker or his allies. They traveled across continents, meeting informants, gaining intelligence, and uncovering hidden connections. Slowly, they pieced together a picture of The Broker's network—an intricate web of associates, assets, and intermediaries.

Their first major lead came from an unexpected source. A former financial analyst for a Luxembourg-based investment firm, who had worked with Consortium members on secretive projects, contacted them through Dr. Moreno's organization. His name was Luca Ferrara, and he had become disillusioned with the corruption he'd witnessed.

"Everything was done through shell companies and offshore accounts," Luca explained, meeting with Maya and Jules in a secluded café in Geneva. "But there was always one name that kept appearing in the background: The Broker. I never met him, but he was like a phantom, his influence everywhere and nowhere."

Maya leaned forward. "Do you have any idea where his assets might be hidden? We're looking for anything that could expose his reach."

Luca nodded slowly. "There's a series of transactions I tracked once, leading to accounts in the Cayman Islands. I kept a record—if The Broker's connected to them, it could lead you closer to his identity."

They took Luca's records and began analyzing the data. It was a painstaking process, but piece by piece, they followed the money trail, uncovering accounts, investments, and properties linked to shell companies spanning the globe. Their investigation pointed to a set of hidden assets in Hong Kong, where The Broker's influence seemed strongest.

Into the Heart of Hong Kong

Maya, Jules, and Henri traveled to Hong Kong, where they began coordinating with trusted contacts to infiltrate The Broker's network. The city was a hub of financial activity, a place where wealth and power coalesced in complex ways, making it an ideal setting for someone as elusive as The Broker.

They identified a key location: a high-rise office building housing a financial management firm that handled investments for some of the world's wealthiest clients. According to Luca's intel, this firm was one of The Broker's primary fronts, allowing him to move assets across borders without detection.

To gather more information, Maya and Jules planned to infiltrate a charity gala hosted by the firm. The event promised to be an exclusive affair, attended by high-profile individuals, many of whom were suspected of having connections to The Broker's operations.

With new identities and credentials forged by Henri, Maya and Jules attended the gala, blending in with the crowd. The event was held in a luxurious ballroom, the glittering chandeliers casting a warm glow over guests dressed in evening wear. They moved through the crowd, listening in on conversations, watching for anyone who might reveal a connection to The Broker.

Near the end of the evening, Jules overheard a conversation between two men at the bar. They spoke in low voices, but she managed to catch fragments:

"—The Broker wants this handled quietly. No more mistakes."

"Agreed. We'll take care of it next week. The last thing we need is more attention."

Jules signaled to Maya, who subtly positioned herself nearby, recording the conversation. This was the confirmation they needed—The Broker was still operating, and he was actively managing his network.

An Unexpected Ally

As they left the gala, a man approached them, his expression tense but determined. He introduced himself as Vincent Cheng, a mid-level associate in the firm who had recognized Maya from a previous exposé on The Consortium. Vincent admitted he was conflicted about his involvement with The Broker's network, but until now, he had felt powerless to act.

"I know things," Vincent said, his voice barely a whisper. "They use us to move money, hide assets, manipulate stocks. If you're serious about taking him down, I'll help you."

Maya and Jules exchanged a look of cautious optimism. Vincent could be the insider they needed, someone who could give them direct access to The Broker's financial empire. But they knew this was risky; Vincent would be putting himself in grave danger by assisting them.

They agreed to meet Vincent the next evening in a safe location, where he provided them with a list of accounts, shell companies, and client names tied to The Broker. Each lead brought them closer to unraveling his financial network, exposing the web of corruption that extended far beyond anything they had seen before.

The Tipping Point

As The Vigilant closed in on The Broker, they faced mounting threats. Vincent went hiding after receiving a series of ominous warnings, while other informants disappeared under suspicious circumstances. It was clear that The Broker was aware of their efforts, and he was willing to do whatever it took to protect his empire.

Determined to see this through, Maya and her team decided on one final, audacious move. They would hack into The Broker's main accounts, exposing his financial transactions in real-time for the world to see. It was a risky strategy—one that could lead to severe repercussions—but they knew it was the only way to ensure The Broker's influence was permanently dismantled.

Raven assembled a team of hackers, each one a trusted ally, to execute the plan. The operation was scheduled for midnight, when financial activity would be minimal, reducing the chance of immediate detection.

As the countdown began, Maya and Jules monitored the operation from their secure base, watching as Raven's team breached The Broker's servers. The first accounts were decrypted within minutes, revealing staggering sums transferred through various shell corporations.

One by one, they exposed transactions, corporate deals, and investments tied to influential figures worldwide. The information spread across social media, news outlets, and financial networks, igniting a frenzy as people realized the depth of The Broker's reach.

The Broker's Response

Just as the operation neared completion, Maya's screen lit up with an incoming call from an unknown number. She answered cautiously, and a familiar voice filled the room.

"Clever move, Maya," The Broker said, his tone cold and calculated. "But do you truly believe this will end me? Power doesn't vanish, it adapts. You've made yourself an enemy of forces you can't even comprehend."

Maya steadied her voice. "Your time is over. You've hidden in the shadows for too long, but now the world knows who you are."

The Broker chuckled, an unsettling sound. "You've won this battle but remember—there are others like me. And we will always find a way back."

Before she could respond, the line went dead. The Broker had escaped once more, but his network was shattered, his finances exposed, his reputation irreparably damaged.

The Aftermath

The global reaction to The Vigilant's latest exposé was unprecedented. Governments launched investigations, private firms severed ties with suspected collaborators, and an international task force was established to pursue any remaining elements of The Broker's network.

Vincent Cheng resurfaced under The Vigilant's protection, his bravery celebrated by activists and journalists alike. He became a symbol of defiance, a testament to the power of courage in the face of corruption.

But Maya knew that The Broker's warning was real. The fight against those who exploited power for personal gain was far from over. Yet, she also knew that The Vigilant had become a force of its own movement that now spanned continents, a beacon for those who refused to accept the status quo.

As Maya stood beside her team, watching the world respond to their latest victory, she felt both a sense of fulfillment and a renewed determination. They had struck a powerful blow, but the journey was only beginning.

With every victory, they grew stronger. And if there were people like The Broker lurking in the shadows, The Vigilant would be there, ready to shine a light and fight for a world that could finally be free from corruption.

For Lily. For The Archivist. For Vincent, Raven, Henri, Jules, and everyone who believed in the power of truth. They were The Vigilant, and their mission had only just begun.

20

Shadows and Allies

The world watched as The Vigilant dismantled the last remnants of The Broker's network. But the farther they reached into the shadows, the more complex the web of corruption became. Even with their recent success, Maya knew there were still countless hidden players, each prepared to do anything to maintain their influence.

An Unexpected Message

A week after The Broker's network was publicly exposed, Maya received an email from an address she didn't recognize. The message was encrypted, bypassing even the most advanced filters The Vigilant had set up. She opened it cautiously.

"Your work has been noticed. You're stirring the world. But beware—when you dig too deep, you may uncover secrets that were never meant to see the light. If you're serious about continuing this mission, meet me in Tokyo. You'll find me in the place where the sakura bloom."

Maya read the message twice, trying to glean any meaning from the cryptic words. She knew it could be a trap, but something about it felt genuine. It sounded like an invitation, but from whom?

She shared the message with Jules, Raven, and Henri. They agreed that, while the risk was high, it could be a valuable opportunity.

"We've come this far," Jules said, her voice resolute. "If there's someone out there who knows about these hidden players, we need to meet them."

With the team's support, Maya prepared to leave for Tokyo, aware that this journey could open doors to new allied enemies.

Arrival in Tokyo

Maya arrived in Tokyo under the guise of a tourist, her movements carefully planned to avoid detection. She had chosen a small hotel in Shinjuku, blending in with the bustling crowds. The city felt both vibrant and secretive, a place where shadows lurked behind neon lights. She thought about the message, "the place where the sakura bloom," and realized it could only mean one thing: Ueno Park, famous for its cherry blossoms.

That evening, as the sun dipped behind the skyline, Maya made her way to the park. She moved carefully, her senses on high alert. The sakura trees were bare in the off-season, their twisted branches casting haunting shadows over the paths.

Just as she neared a secluded area, a figure stepped out from behind a tree. The man appeared to be in his fifties, his hair graying at the temples, his posture calm yet guarded. He nodded to her, his gaze piercing.

"You must be Maya," he said, his voice low.

Maya studied him, trying to gauge his intentions. "And you are?"

"They call me Kaido," he replied. "I'm a former operative. I once worked in intelligence, until I realized the price of loyalty to hidden powers."

She nodded, still wary. "You sent the message?"

He inclined his head. "Yes. I've been following your work, Maya. The Vigilant is changing the world in ways I once dreamed of. But you've only scratched the surface."

Maya felt a surge of curiosity. "So, what do you know?"

Kaido gestured to a nearby bench, indicating that she should sit. "There's a network beyond The Consortium. They operate through multiple fronts, often invisible to anyone outside their inner circle. The Broker was only a manager, a handler for these larger players. They're the ones truly orchestrating things—the architects of chaos."

He handed her a USB drive. "This contains information on some of their key operatives, their methods, and their targets. But be warned: they won't hesitate to retaliate. If you continue this path, you'll be stepping into a war far darker than anything you've faced before.

Maya took the drive, her heart pounding. "Why are you helping us?"

Kaido's gaze softened. "Because I've seen what happens when these people go unchecked. I spent my career serving them, following orders without question. I've watched good people disappear; honest voices silenced. I couldn't save them then, but maybe I can help you now."

She nodded, grateful yet wary. "And what happens if they find out you've given us this?"

A faint smile crossed his lips. "I accepted the risk long ago. But be careful, Maya. They're watching you."

Return to Headquarters

Maya returned to her hotel and immediately reached out to Jules and the team, arranging a secure line to transfer the contents of Kaido's drive. The files were vast, containing dossiers, communications, and financial transactions, enough information to confirm Kaido's claims. It was a revelation that shook The Vigilant to its core: they were up against something far more organized, far more entrenched than they'd imagined.

The group held a virtual meeting, where they reviewed the findings together. Raven's eyes widened as she scanned through the documents.

"This is… staggering," she said. "They have assets in nearly every sector—media, tech, pharmaceuticals, even NGOs. They're influencing policy, manipulating markets. This isn't just corruption; it's control."

Henri looked grim. "If we go after them, they'll retaliate harder than ever. But if we don't, they'll continue to operate unchecked."

Maya felt the weight of their decision pressing on her. They had taken down The Consortium, but this was something larger, a deeply rooted network capable of operating from behind the scenes. Kaido's files had provided names, locations, and operations, but taking down this group would require resources they had never used before.

"We need allies," Maya said finally. "More than ever. If we're going to confront them, we can't do it alone."

The Global Alliance

In the following weeks, The Vigilant reached out to every trusted contact, journalist, whistleblower, and former intelligence officer they could find. With Kaido's files as leverage, they managed to secure partnerships with activists, human rights organizations, and government insiders who had long suspected the existence of such a network but lacked the evidence to act.

Dr. Sofia Moreno, a steadfast ally, led the diplomatic efforts, meeting with international leaders who could lend their support discreetly. Through her work, they gained access to diplomatic channels and intelligence networks, providing them with a degree of protection and insight.

The Vigilant expanded its operations, setting up decentralized hubs in multiple countries. They trained new recruits, implemented advanced encryption, and reinforced their defenses. This time, they weren't just exposing corruption, they were going to war with a hidden empire.

Operation Obsidian

As The Vigilant planned its assault on the network, they devised a strategy called Operation Obsidian. Their goal was to target the core pillars of the organization: finance, media influence, and global policy manipulation. By destabilizing these pillars, they could weaken the network's grip on power, making it vulnerable to exposure.

Finance: Raven led a team to track and freeze the network's assets, working closely with international financial regulators. By cutting off the flow of money, they hoped to cripple the organization's operations.

Media Influence: Jules and a group of investigative journalists set out to expose the media entities owned or influenced by the network. They planned to reveal how these outlets shaped public opinion, manipulated narratives, and silenced dissenting voices.

Global Policy: Henri and Dr. Moreno focused on gathering evidence of policy manipulation, working with government officials to expose key players who had been bribed or blackmailed into furthering the network's agenda.

Each phase of Operation Obsidian required precision and secrecy. They coordinated with allies around the world, ensuring that each strike would be synchronized, hitting the network at its weakest points.

The First Strikes

The initial phase of Operation Obsidian was launched with strategic precision. Within days, several of the network's major financial accounts were frozen, and investigations into compromised media outlets gained traction. News stories began emerging, connecting high-profile figures to shadowy transactions and backroom deals.

The public response was explosive. Protests erupted globally, demanding accountability and transparency from governments and corporations. The network scrambled to contain the fallout, but The Vigilant's evidence was too damning to ignore.

Jules and her team released a series of exposés, detailing how certain media conglomerates had manipulated information to favor powerful interests. The revelations caused a massive loss of trust, leading to boycotts, resignations, and calls for reform.

For the first time, the network's operatives were forced into the open, scrambling to protect their assets. And as the walls closed in, Maya received a message from Kaido:

"You're making progress, but beware—The Broker was only one of many. They're more resilient than you think."

The Backlash

As The Vigilant celebrated their victories, a powerful counterattack struck. Cyber-attacks hit their secure servers, and several of their informants went silent, likely forced into hiding. Threatening messages appeared, warning of dire consequences if they continued their pursuit.

Raven's team worked tirelessly to secure their systems, but Maya knew that each day the network would adapt, finding new ways to attack. Their enemy was not just a single organization, but a complex, adaptable machine designed to survive in secrecy.

A Battle Far from Over

Maya gathered her team, her voice steady but filled with conviction. "We've exposed part of this network, but Kaido's right—they're far from defeated. They'll regroup, they'll change tactics, and they'll come after us harder than ever. But we have something they don't."

Jules looked at her, understanding. "The truth. And we have the people on our side."

Maya nodded. "As long as we're willing to fight, if we have allies, they'll never silence us. We're The Vigilant, and this mission isn't just about one victory. It's about holding power accountable, no matter the cost."

The team stood together, resolutely aware of the dangers yet united by their shared purpose. They had come this far, and they would continue, undeterred by the threats that loomed.

As Maya looked out at her team, she felt a deep, unwavering resolve. This was a battle that would require everything they had, but she knew that if there were shadows to uncover, The Vigilant would be there, shining a light for the world to see.

Their journey was far from over, but together, they were ready for whatever came next.

21

The Price of Truth

With each victory, The Vigilant had grown stronger, their influence spread across borders, their reach expanding as new allies joined their cause. Yet every step forward came at a cost. As Maya, Jules, and their team struck blow after blow against the hidden powers, they knew that their enemy was preparing to retaliate in ways that went beyond physical threats.

A Silent Threat

One evening, as Maya prepared her latest briefing on the network's activities, an unexpected notification appeared on her screen. Her personal bank account had been frozen, flagged for "suspicious activity." A moment later, another alert informed her that her identification records had been flagged for review, effectively erasing her identity in several critical systems. Medical records, property ownership, travel history—gone, as if she had never existed.

Maya felt a cold realization settle over her. This was a new tactic. Instead of targeting her physically, the network was systematically erasing her existence.

She immediately contacted Jules, who had already received similar notifications. Their phones, emails, even secure accounts were all locked, flagged, or deleted. In mere moments, The Vigilant's leaders had become ghosts, stripped of their digital identities, isolated from their resources.

"This is different," Maya murmured, her voice tense as she scanned the data. "They're using our own systems against us."

Jules clenched her fists, anger simmering in her eyes. "They're not just trying to stop us—they're trying to erase us."

The team quickly went into crisis mode, contacting Raven and Henri, who confirmed that similar issues were affecting members across their global network. The message was clear: the hidden powers were using their influence to systematically dismantle The Vigilant from within, one identity at a time.

Kaido's Intervention

As Maya struggled to regain access to her accounts, a message appeared on her screen from Kaido. His words were short but direct:

"Meet me in Hong Kong. I have resources that can help you. But this is the last time I can assist."

The urgency in his message was undeniable. Maya understood that Kaido, too, was taking a significant risk by aiding them. She arranged for a covert flight, while Jules and Henri coordinated with the remaining team to keep operations running as best they could.

When she arrived in Hong Kong, Kaido led her through a maze of backstreets, eventually guiding her to a small, nondescript building. Inside was a secure room filled with high-tech equipment, encrypted devices, and several screens showing real-time data feeds.

Kaido motioned for her to sit, then activated a secure line. "You're dealing with people who have mastered the art of digital warfare. They don't need to target you physically to destroy you; they only need to erase your existence."

Maya nodded, feeling the weight of his words. "So, what can we do?"

Kaido handed her a small device, a portable drive loaded with encrypted files. "This will help you restore some of your digital footprint. But more importantly, it contains a list of safe contacts—people within intelligence, tech, and finance who are sympathetic to your cause. You'll need them to rebuild what's been lost."

Maya took the drive, gratitude in her eyes. "Thank you, Kaido. I know the risks you're taking."

Kaido's expression softened. "I believe in what you're doing, Maya. But understand—this network, these people... they will not stop until they've erased every trace of your mission. You must be relentless."

Rebuilding from the Ground Up

Back at their hidden base, Maya used Kaido's drive to restore what she could of her and Jules' identities. It was a painstaking process, piecing together fragments of digital data, rebuilding bank accounts, restoring access to encrypted files. With the help of Kaido's contacts, they managed to establish new identities, new accounts, and new secure lines.

But it wasn't enough to simply exist. They needed to act, to show their enemies that The Vigilant could not be erased so easily.

Maya called a meeting with the remaining team, laying out a bold plan to target the network's own digital infrastructure. "They've shown us how they operate," she began, her voice steady. "Now we're going to use their own tactics against them."

Jules nodded, a spark of determination in her eyes. "We infiltrate their systems, expose their hidden servers, and disrupt their operations. If they want to play this game, we'll show them that we're not backing down."

With Kaido's contacts and Raven's team of cyber experts, The Vigilant launched a counteroffensive. They hacked into several key servers, exposing encrypted communications and financial transactions that linked the network to prominent corporations and government officials. The information was damning, implicating figures who had long remained above suspicion.

The Public Response

The release of the hacked documents spread like wildfire. News outlets and social media were flooded with information about the hidden network's manipulation of global markets, the influence it wielded over major institutions, and the corrupt deals that had kept it thriving. The backlash was immediate, with calls for investigations, arrests, and an overhaul of systems vulnerable to such exploitation.

But the response wasn't limited to public outrage. Allies and supporters of The Vigilant rallied worldwide, organizing protests, demanding accountability, and forming new coalitions to protect journalists, activists, and whistleblowers.

Maya felt a renewed sense of hope. For every powerful figure trying to silence them, there were hundreds of voices rising in support. The Vigilant had sparked a movement, a wave of people willing to fight for transparency and justice.

But they also knew that the network's response would be swift and merciless.

The Cost of Defiance

In the days following the counteroffensive, The Vigilant faced a series of coordinated attacks. Their safe houses were compromised, forcing the team to relocate frequently. Several informants and whistleblowers were threatened, and in some cases, disappeared without a trace.

One night, Maya received a call from an encrypted line. She recognized the voice immediately—it was The Broker.

"You're playing with forces you don't understand, Maya," he said, his tone calm but filled with menace. "Do you think the world cares about your crusade? People want stability and comfort. You threaten that with every secret you expose."

Maya's voice was steady. "People deserve the truth. They deserve to know who's pulling the strings."

The Broker chuckled darkly. "Perhaps. But remember—power has a way of surviving. You've become a nuisance, Maya, and nuisances are dealt with."

The line went dead, but the threat lingered.

A Race Against Time

Realizing that their enemy was closing in, Maya and Jules accelerated their plans. They worked day and night, gathering as much evidence as possible, coordinating with allies around the world to create a failsafe: a massive data dump that would go public in the event of their capture or death. Every piece of information they had uncovered, every document, every name, was uploaded to secure servers, programmed to release should they fail to enter a code every 48 hours.

It was a drastic measure, but Maya knew it was necessary. They were fighting against time, against an enemy with resources that could outlast them, and they needed to ensure their mission would continue, even if they couldn't.

The Alliance Grows Stronger

In the face of adversity, The Vigilant's alliance continued to grow. Kaido's contacts provided valuable intelligence, Dr. Moreno rallied diplomatic support, and Raven's team fortified their cyber defenses. They were no longer just a team of whistleblowers and activists; they had become a global coalition, a force capable of challenging even the most deeply entrenched powers.

Maya and Jules worked tirelessly, holding virtual meetings, coordinating strikes, and training new recruits. The Vigilant network was now spread across multiple continents, each cell operating independently yet aligned with the same mission: to dismantle corruption, no matter where it hid.

In a final act of defiance, Maya arranged a public broadcast, calling out the shadowy network by name, exposing their methods, and rallying people to stand against them.

"The world deserves to know who's truly in control," she said, her voice firm. "We are The Vigilant, and we will not stop until justice is served."

The Battle of Influence

The network responded with a final, desperate move. They launched a smear campaign against The Vigilant, planting false stories, manipulating news cycles, and paying off journalists to discredit Maya and her team. It was a coordinated attack on their reputation, designed to undermine their credibility and turn public opinion against them.

But Maya and her allies were prepared. With their vast collection of evidence, they released a new wave of documents, showcasing the network's reach into media, politics, and finance. Every lie was countered with irrefutable proof, every smear with hard evidence.

The battle raged on in headlines, on social media, in courtrooms. But each attempt to silence The Vigilant only brought more attention to their cause, more people questioning the status quo.

A Lasting Legacy

As the dust began to settle, Maya reflected on the cost of their mission. They had lost allies, friends, and nearly everything that defined them. But in the end, they had created something that would endure. The world had changed; The Vigilant had proven that even the most powerful could be held accountable, that truth could prevail over fear.

Maya looked at her team, the people who had sacrificed everything for a vision of justice and felt a surge of pride. They had become more than an organization—they were a movement, a symbol of defiance against the forces that sought to control and exploit.

And if there were people willing to stand up, The Vigilant would endure a legacy of courage, resilience, and truth.

The battle was far from over, but Maya knew that, together, they had already changed the world. For Lily. For The Archivist. For every voice silenced, and for every truth yet to be revealed.

22

Echoes of Resistance

In the weeks following their last confrontation with the shadowy network, The Vigilant settled into a tense but determined rhythm. The public support they had garnered was strong, but so was the pushback. Across the world, governments and corporations were forced to confront uncomfortable truths, while members of The Vigilant remained in constant motion, anticipating the next strike from their enemies.

Maya had grown accustomed to a life of vigilance, but the toll it took on her team was undeniable. Their work had brought justice, but it had also brought danger, sacrifice, and loss. As she looked around at her exhausted but resolute allies, she knew she needed to find a way to sustain them in the long fight ahead.

A New Vision for The Vigilant

One night, after a particularly grueling strategy meeting, Maya gathered her core team—Jules, Henri, Raven, and Dr. Sofia Moreno—to discuss the future. She had a vision, one that had been forming in her mind since Kaido's final warning. It was time to evolve.

"We've been on the defensive for too long," Maya began. "But I believe we can do more than just expose corruption. We have the support, the allies, the network to create a system that protects truth and justice. A foundation that will endure, even when we're gone."

Jules looked at her thoughtfully. "You're talking about something permanent—a true global network that outlasts any one of us."

Maya nodded. "Yes. We've been The Vigilant, a reaction to the darkness we've uncovered. But now we need to create something stronger, something proactive. We need to be a coalition that not only exposes corruption but actively works to prevent it.

Dr. Moreno leaned forward, her eyes bright with interest. "A foundation, a force for accountability. Something to counterbalance these hidden powers."

They spent the rest of the night discussing logistics: a decentralized organization that combined journalism, advocacy, and legal aid, one that would train activists, protect whistleblowers, and coordinate with trusted allies worldwide. It would be called The Foundation, and its mission would be to hold power accountable, provide safe channels for truth-tellers, and empower communities affected by corruption.

Building The Foundation

The next few months were a whirlwind of activity. The Vigilant transformed into The Foundation, with new recruits and allies rallying to their cause. Kaido's contacts proved invaluable, connecting them with experts in cybersecurity, legal protections, and political advocacy. Their new organization grew rapidly, with cells in over a dozen countries, each operating autonomously but aligned in purpose.

One of their first initiatives was a Whistleblower Protection Program, designed to provide safe passage, legal defense, and financial support for those willing to come forward with evidence of corruption or abuse. They created secure platforms for journalists to share their findings, encrypted servers to protect sensitive data, and crisis teams ready to relocate high-risk individuals at a moment's notice.

Jules took the lead on The Foundation's media initiatives, working to restore public trust in the press by promoting transparency and ethical journalism. Henri focused on organizing a network of legal experts and former intelligence officers to support whistleblowers and activists in hostile regions. Dr. Moreno coordinated outreach programs to empower affected communities, ensuring that The Foundation's mission resonated with everyday people.

Maya continued to work at the heart of the organization, overseeing operations, coordinating with allies, and strategizing new ways to disrupt the remnants of the hidden network that still loomed in the shadows.

The Return of The Broker

Just as The Foundation gained momentum, Maya received an encrypted message on her personal line. It was from an anonymous source, but the signature was unmistakable. The Broker was reaching out again.

"You've come far, Maya. But you're still only minor disruption in a much larger game. If you wish to survive, you'll need to know what you're truly up against. Meet me in Vienna. Alone."

Maya felt a surge of apprehension. The Broker's influence had been diminished, but his network was far from destroyed. She knew meeting him could be a trap, yet there was an allure in understanding her enemy. If he was reaching out, it meant he needed something—a weakness she might exploit.

She shared the message with Jules and Henri, who were immediately concerned.

"It could be a trap," Jules warned. "He's a master of manipulation. He might be trying to bait you into a situation where he has the advantage."

Maya considered this, but her instincts told her there was more to the invitation. "He's been on the run since we dismantled The Consortium, and he's losing allies fast. If he's reaching out, it means he's desperate. I need to see what he knows."

After some discussion, they agreed on a plan. Maya would meet The Broker in Vienna, but she wouldn't be alone. Raven and a small team would follow from a distance, ready to intervene if things turned out to be dangerous.

The Meeting in Vienna

Maya arrived in Vienna and made her way to a secluded café in the city's historic district. The Broker was waiting for her at a back table, looking remarkably composed, a slight smirk on his face as she approached.

"Ah, Maya. I was beginning to wonder if you'd lost your nerve," he greeted, his voice smooth and confident.

Maya kept her expression neutral as she took a seat across from him. "You reached out to me. So, tell me—what's the game this time?"

The Broker studied her, his eyes sharp and calculating. "You've become a powerful adversary. I respect that. But surely you know that true power doesn't lie in winning battles. It's in controlling the battlefield."

He leaned forward, lowering his voice. "You think you've disrupted the network, but you've only grazed the surface. There's a structure for older and more resilient than you realize, operating through connections you haven't even considered."

Maya felt a flicker of unease but kept her gaze steady. "Then why tell me this? What do you want?"

The Broker's smirk faded, replaced by a look of quiet intensity. "I want you to understand that you're playing a dangerous game, Maya. The ones truly in power are not just individuals, their institutions, ideologies. They don't die with one man's arrest. You'll need more than idealism and courage to fight them. You'll need allies, resources, and above all, strategy."

He handed her a small notebook, filled with names and locations she recognized as key figures and sites tied to The Foundation's mission.

"These are players who could help you—or destroy you, depending on how you approach them. Consider this my parting gift," he said, his voice laced with something close to respect. "I've done my part. Now, it's your move."

Maya took the notebook, a cold understanding settling over her. The Broker wasn't offering help of kindness; he was offering a warning, a reminder that the battle was larger than either of them.

As she rose to leave, he leaned back, a faint smile on his lips. "Good luck, Maya. I suspect you'll need it."

A Broader War

Back at headquarters, Maya shared The Broker's notebook with her team. Each name, each place, represented a new facet of their fighting international banking heads, tech moguls, military contractors, and more. It was an ecosystem of influence, one that thrived on secrecy and mutual interests, bound by power rather than loyalty.

Henri spoke first, his expression thoughtful. "He's right about one thing: this goes far deeper than any of us realized."

Jules nodded, a determined glint in her eyes. "But now we know their connections, their strongholds. We can prepare, anticipate their moves."

Maya placed the notebook on the table, her resolve solidified. "We're going to need more than just information. We'll need allies, global partnerships, and support from people who believe in what we're doing.

They set to work, mobilizing The Foundation's network, reaching out to allies in government, finance, and human rights organizations. They held confidential meetings, shared intelligence, and gained the support of influential figures who could protect them from the backlash they knew would come.

The Final Standoff

As The Foundation's influence grew, so did the tension. The hidden powers began to fight back, launching cyber-attacks, discrediting campaigns, and covertly threatening their allies. In response, Maya and her team doubled their efforts, focusing on transparency, rallying public support, and exposing every attack for the world to see.

One night, as Maya reviewed a final report detailing the network's vulnerabilities, she felt a sense of calm resolve to settle over her. This was the culmination of everything they had worked for—the truth laid bare, the shadowed figures exposed, a world on the brink of change.

The next morning, The Foundation launched a coordinated release of information, implicating top officials, financiers, and corporate leaders. The exposé dominated headlines, sparking protests, investigations, and, finally, policy reforms. Public pressure forced governments to act, and one by one, the power structures that had long operated in darkness began to crumble.

A Legacy of Light

As the dust settled, Maya reflected on the journey that had brought them here. The world had changed, shaped by the courage of those willing to stand for the truth. The Foundation had become more than an organization—it was a symbol, a promise that power would be held accountable, that justice could prevail even in the darkest of times.

Their work was far from finished. Corruption would continue, new threats would emerge, and the fight for truth would never truly end. But they had shown that the impossible was achievable, that light could reach even the deepest shadows.

Standing beside her team, Maya felt a profound sense of purpose, a resolve that had only grown stronger. They had built a legacy, one that would endure as long as there were people willing to fight for it.

They were The Foundation, a movement dedicated to truth, justice, and the unbreakable belief that the world could, and should, be better.

And for the first time, Maya allowed herself to hope—for a future where their work might one day be complete, a future forged by every truth they had brought to light.

23

A World Remade

The exposé shook the foundations of global power. The Foundation's revelations led to resignations, trials, and systemic reform efforts in countries around the world. No longer hidden behind veils of secrecy, the elite networks of corruption and manipulation faced scrutiny like never before. Public outcry turned into organized movements, and allies of The Foundation emerged from unexpected places, pledging support to the mission Maya and her team had championed for so long.

But Maya knew that the end of one battle only meant the beginning of another. With the global impact of their work came new challenges, new threats, and an urgent need to adapt.

A New Enemy

As The Foundation gained influence, a new kind of adversary began to surface. This was no shadowy figure lurking behind closed doors; it was a public entity coalition of corporations, powerful individuals, and political groups uniting to resist The Foundation's growing influence. Calling themselves "The Collective," they branded their mission as a defense of "freedom from tyranny," painting The Foundation as an unchecked force that threatened personal freedoms and global stability.

The Collective used the media to sway public opinion, portraying The Foundation as an invasive force pushing its own agenda. They hired PR firms to plant articles, circulated op-eds, and even staged protests, casting doubt on the legitimacy of The Foundation's work. Public opinion grew divided, with some questioning whether Maya and her team were overstepping boundaries in their pursuit of justice.

In response, The Foundation held public forums, issued transparent reports, and increased outreach to communities worldwide. They worked with journalists to expose The Collective's motivations, revealing its backers to be powerful figures who had profited from the very systems of corruption The Foundation had fought to dismantle.

But Maya could see that the battle for truth had grown more complex. She realized that to maintain trust, The Foundation needed to evolve once again, this time into something even more resilient.

An Offer from Kaido

One evening, Maya received an unexpected message from Kaido, who had gone underground after their last encounter. This time, he requested a video call. When Maya connected, Kaido appeared on the screen, his face shadowed but calm.

"Maya," he began, his tone serious. "You've disrupted the power balance, and now the backlash has begun. The Foundation is strong, but The Collective will use every resource they have to undermine you. If you're going to survive this, you'll need to become something they can't easily attack."

Maya listened carefully. "What are you suggesting?"

Kaido leaned forward. "I've been working on something—an autonomous network, a secure system that can operate independently of any one individual or location. It's a decentralized platform that would allow you to run The Foundation from anywhere, making it nearly impossible to trace or dismantle."

He pulled up a schematic of the system, explaining how the network would work as a series of encrypted nodes scattered worldwide. Each node would operate independently yet contribute to the whole, ensuring that even if one part was compromised, the rest would remain secure.

"It's called The Nexus," Kaido continued. "With it, The Foundation will be everywhere and nowhere. No headquarters, no centralized control, no single point of weakness."

Maya felt a surge of excitement mixed with caution. This could change everything. With The Nexus, The Foundation could operate with unprecedented freedom, unhindered by physical or digital attacks. But it would also mean a complete restructuring of their organization.

"Kaido," she said slowly, "this could work. But can it be done?"

Kaido nodded, his gaze steady. "It can. But it will require absolute commitment from everyone involved. The Foundation will need to let go of traditional structures. You'll be a network of allies rather than a single organization."

Maya looked at Jules, Henri, and Raven, who had joined the call. Each of them wore expressions of determination and resolve. They knew the risks, but they also knew this was their best chance to keep their work alive.

"Let's do it," Maya said, her voice filled with purpose. "We'll become The Nexus."

The Transformation

Over the next several months, Maya and her team worked tirelessly to transition The Foundation into The Nexus. The process was complex, requiring coordination between dozens of cells worldwide, each tasked with securing independent nodes that could operate autonomously yet remain part of the larger network.

The Nexus was built on Kaido's design, with encrypted nodes and decentralized communication hubs that allowed members to connect, share information, and coordinate actions without risking exposure. The Nexus was structured to be leaderless, with decisions made collectively by trusted operatives. This shift required a new level of adaptability and trust, but it also meant that no single person or cell could be targeted or dismantled.

As The Nexus took shape, The Collective ramped up its attacks. They intensified their media campaign, portraying The Nexus as a rogue network operating outside the law. But Maya and her team anticipated this, and every false accusation was met with transparent evidence to the contrary, showing that The Nexus remained true to its mission of exposing corruption and protecting truth.

And as The Collective fought back, the resilience of The Nexus became clear. With each attempt to discredit or dismantle them, The Nexus adapted, drawing strength from its decentralized structure and the growing support of people who believed in their cause.

The People's Network

As The Nexus grew, it became more than just a network of operatives. Everyday people began to join in, inspired by The Nexus's work and willing to act as local nodes, providing shelter, resources, and support for those in need. Communities that had once been powerless now found themselves empowered, contributing to The Nexus's mission by reporting corruption, protecting whistleblowers, and supporting journalists who dared to seek the truth.

One evening, Maya received a message from a local organizer in Brazil, who shared a story of a young woman who had exposed corruption in her local government thanks to support from The Nexus. In another message, a group of activists in Nigeria reported that they had formed a network to protect journalists from government retaliation, inspired by The Nexus's resilience.

Maya felt a deep sense of purpose and pride. The Nexus had become a force that extended beyond her and her team, a global movement of ordinary people standing up for truth. They were no longer just an organization; they were a network of allies, a testament to the power of collective action.

A Final Confrontation with The Collective

The Collective, frustrated by its inability to dismantle The Nexus, began resorting to drastic measures. They hired mercenaries, launched targeted cyber-attacks, and even attempted to infiltrate The Nexus by planting spies. But each attempt was met with fierce resistance, as The Nexus's decentralized structure made it nearly impossible to compromise the entire network.

Realizing that they could not defeat The Nexus through conventional means, The Collective tried a new approach: they issued a direct challenge to Maya and her team, offering a truce in exchange for negotiations. They claimed they wanted to "restore balance" and proposed a meeting on neutral ground.

Maya knew it was likely a trap, but she also saw an opportunity to confront The Collective face-to-face, to call out their actions and expose their hypocrisy. After consulting with her team, she agreed to the meeting, choosing a highly visible location where any action against her would be witnessed by the public.

The meeting took place in a neutral country, in a public park under heavy surveillance. Maya arrived with Jules, Henri, and Raven, prepared for anything. Across from them stood three representatives of The Collective—polished, powerful, and unflinchingly confident.

"We're offering you a way out, Maya," one of them said smoothly. "You can step down, dissolve this network of yours, and return to a normal life. No more threats, no more battles. You've made your point."

Maya held her ground, her gaze unwavering. "A way out? You mean a way back into the shadows? That's not an option. We've exposed the truth, and we won't stop until every hidden power you've abused is brought to light."

The Collective's representatives exchanged glances, their expressions hardening. "You're playing a dangerous game, Maya. Power is a tide—it can recede, but it always returns. Your network may be strong now, but eventually, people will tire of your crusade. They'll forget. And when that happens, we'll be here, waiting."

Maya's voice was steady as she replied. "Power may return, but so will the people. And they'll be stronger, more vigilant. Because now they know what you're capable of."

The Collective representatives remained silent for a moment, then turned and left, their message delivered. But Maya knew they were wrong. The Collective might regroup, might attempt to rebuild their influence, but they would never again operate without scrutiny.

A New Dawn

As Maya returned to her team, she felt a sense of closure. They had faced down The Collective, showing the world that corruption and manipulation would always be met with resistance. And now, The Nexus was a beacon, a global network that would continue the work, regardless of who led it.

In the days that followed, The Nexus expanded even further, with communities around the world taking ownership of the movement. They trained new leaders, empowered local voices, and created a self-sustaining network that would carry on the fight for transparency, accountability, and justice.

Maya, Jules, Henri, and Raven gathered for a quiet moment, reflecting on everything they had accomplished. They knew that their mission was far from over, but they also knew that they had created something enduring, something that could stand against any force that tried to silence it.

As dawn broke over their hidden headquarters, Maya felt a deep sense of peace. They had built not only a movement but a legacy—one that would endure long after they were gone.

The world had changed, and it would continue to change. For Lily. For The Archivist. For every truth that had been hidden and every voice that had been silenced.

The Nexus would live on, an unstoppable force of truth in a world forever altered.

24

The Echoes of Legacy

As The Nexus solidified its influence and continued its work, Maya found herself drawn into a new role—one she hadn't anticipated. She was no longer just a leader; she was now a symbol of resilience, her name synonymous with truth and defiance. Allies across the globe, from journalists to activists to ordinary citizens, looked to her not only for guidance but also for inspiration.

But with this new status came a quiet burden. She realized that she was now as much a target as The Nexus itself. While she had led from the front lines, her visibility had made it dangerous to remain so accessible. She needed to transition, to empower others to carry on The Nexus's mission without her constant oversight.

One evening, as she reviewed a dossier on emerging Nexus leaders, she received a message from Kaido, her longtime ally and the architect behind The Nexus's decentralized structure. His message was short, but it held a depth that spoke volumes:

"It's time to let them lead."

Maya felt a pang of resistance—The Nexus was her life's work, her purpose. But Kaido was right. The strength of The Nexus lay in its ability to function without reliance on any single individual, even her. She knew the time had come to pass the torch, to ensure that The Nexus could endure independently.

Training the Next Generation

Over the following months, Maya and her team focused on developing the next generation of leaders within The Nexus. They selected individuals from diverse backgrounds—whistleblowers, activists, cybersecurity experts, former intelligence operatives, and grassroots organizers. Each one had proven their dedication to The Nexus's cause, and each brought a unique skill set to the table.

Maya personally trained several of them, teaching them the tactics, values, and resilience that had guided her through years of fighting against seemingly insurmountable odds. She shared her knowledge, her strategies, and even her own failures, ensuring that they understood the cost of leadership and the importance of integrity.

Jules, Henri, and Raven joined her in these efforts, each providing specialized training. Jules taught media strategy and public relations, equipping the new leaders to navigate misinformation and protect The Nexus's reputation. Henri focused on operational security and crisis management, ensuring they could handle emergencies with composure. Raven, as always, taught them to see in the shadows, to anticipate threats before they surface.

Through this rigorous training, The Nexus evolved. It was no longer a single network but a constellation of independent cells, each capable of functioning autonomously yet connected by shared principles and purpose.

A Farewell to the Front Lines

As the new leaders took on greater responsibilities, Maya slowly began to step back from day-to-day operations. She no longer led every mission, no longer directed every strategy. Instead, she became an advisor, a guiding force that offered support from the sidelines while allowing others to step into the spotlight.

One evening, after a successful mission that exposed a global money-laundering scheme tied to former allies of The Collective, Maya gathered her core team in a quiet moment of reflection.

"It's strange," she admitted, looking around at Jules, Henri, Raven, and the emerging leaders. "For so long, I was afraid of what would happen if I stepped back. I thought that The Nexus depended on me. But now, seeing all of you, I realize that it's stronger than ever because it no longer needs any one of us."

Jules nodded; her eyes filled with pride. "That was always the goal, wasn't it? To create something that could stand on its own, something that no one person could control or destroy."

Henri raised a glass. "To The Nexus. And to a future where the fight for truth is in the hands of everyone, not just a few."

They clinked their glasses, sharing a moment of gratitude, aware of the journey they had shared and the battles they had won together. They knew they would remain allies, friends, and family, but this was also the beginning of a new chapter.

A World Transformed

As Maya continued to step back, The Nexus grew even more influential. Each independent cell adapted to its local context, taking on issues specific to their regions while staying connected to the broader mission. In Latin America, The Nexus exposed human rights abuses; in Eastern Europe, they fought government corruption; in Southeast Asia, they confronted illegal corporate practices that threatened communities.

People everywhere found courage in The Nexus's example. Communities organized themselves, creating their own small Nexus-inspired groups to hold local authorities accountable. The idea of transparency, accountability, and community-driven justice became not just the domain of activists but a way of life for ordinary citizens who wanted a better world.

Maya watched from afar, deeply moved. The Nexus was no longer an organization, it had become a philosophy, a global movement that empowered people to take ownership of their societies, to stand against injustice no matter where it appeared.

The Final Message from Kaido

One day, Maya received a package from Kaido. Inside was a single letter, written in his precise, almost artistic handwriting:

"Maya, you've done more than you set out to achieve. The Nexus is unstoppable now, a force woven into the fabric of a changing world. But remember, there will always be new forms of power, new shadows that will try to reassert control. This is the nature of our struggle. The only way to win is to ensure the fight lives on through others.

"I have taken my own path now, knowing that The Nexus is in capable hands. You have not only created a legacy; you have given the world a gift that will endure beyond us. And that, Maya, is true power."

Maya felt a mixture of sorrow and pride as she read his words. Kaido, her mysterious and steadfast ally, had moved on. She knew she might never hear from him again, but his influence, his wisdom, would always be a part of The Nexus—and a part of her.

A Quiet Life, A Lasting Impact

Months turned into years. Maya settled into a quieter life, away from the front lines, yet always watching, always ready to support The Nexus if needed. She spent her days writing, documenting her experiences, her thoughts, and the lessons she had learned. Her writings became a guidebook of sorts for future generations of activists and leaders, a testament to the journey that had shaped her.

Jules took on a more public role, becoming a visible face for The Nexus, a voice that continued to speak out, to inspire, and to rally people worldwide. Henri and Raven continued their work behind the scenes, advising and mentoring new leaders as The Nexus expanded into regions they had once thought unreachable.

And though Maya had stepped back, her legacy lived on in every action The Nexus took, in every voice it empowered, and in every truth it defended. She watched as her vision became a reality far greater than she had ever imagined.

A World Changed Forever

In the years that followed, The Nexus became a central part of the global landscape. Its influence extended into schools, governments, media, and communities. The concept of transparency and accountability became an expectation rather than an exception, woven into the policies and values of societies around the world. The Nexus had shifted the balance of power, ensuring that corruption could no longer thrive in the shadows without challenge.

The Collective, now a faint memory, had faded into obscurity, their influence eroded by the unstoppable momentum of The Nexus. The structures of power that had once seemed unbreakable were now subject to the scrutiny of a world powered by truth.

And Maya, though she had retreated from the public eye, remained a living legend—a symbol of resilience, courage, and the unyielding pursuit of justice.

Epilogue: The Legacy of Maya and The Nexus

Years after Maya had left the front lines, a young journalist visited her, seeking to understand the origins of The Nexus. They sat together on a quiet evening, the journalist's recorder running as Maya recounted the journey from The Vigilant to The Nexus, the battles they had fought, the people they had lost, and the vision that had driven them all.

"Did you ever imagine it would grow this far?" the journalist asked, awe in their voice.

Maya smiled; her gaze distant but filled with warmth. "In my heart, I hoped it would. But it wasn't about what I imagined or what any one of us could do alone. The Nexus isn't just an organization; it's a testament to the strength of people who believe in each other, who believe in truth. That's what makes it unstoppable."

The journalist paused, considering her words. "So, what's next for The Nexus? What would you say to the people who are carrying it forward now?"

Maya's eyes sparkled, her voice steady. "I would tell them to never stop questioning, to never lose sight of why they started. The world will always have shadows, but if there are people willing to stand up, to challenge, to believe in something greater than themselves, there will always be hope."

As the interview ended and the journalist left, Maya watched the sun set over the horizon, feeling quiet satisfaction. The work was never finished, but she knew that her part had been fulfilled.

For Lily. For The Archivist. For every voice that had joined them, and for every truth that had been brought to light.

The Nexus would live on if there were people willing to carry its mission forward. And for Maya, that was enough.

25

Passing the Torch

Years had passed since Maya had taken a step back from The Nexus. The organization was now fully autonomous, thriving under the leadership of new voices, younger generations of activists, and allies across the world. She was proud of what they had built—an entity that outgrew its founders and became a living movement.

But as The Nexus expanded, new challenges arose, each generation encountering fresh complexities. The political landscape had changed, with technology advancing at an unprecedented rate, bringing both empowerment and threats. Old adversaries evolved, and new threats emerged in ways no one had anticipated. Even though The Nexus was resilient, Maya sensed that it was time for the next generation to understand the essence that had brought them all together.

And so, Maya decided to do something she hadn't before: she would gather the core team one last time.

A Reunion of Allies

Maya sent messages to the original members of The Nexus's core team—Jules, Henri, Raven, and Dr. Sofia Moreno. Each had gone on to lead their own initiatives, some in public and some in private, yet their bond remained. The invitation was simple: a meeting in person, a rare occurrence given their high-profile pasts and the network's insistence on security.

They chose a remote retreat in the Swiss Alps, far from the reach of digital surveillance, where they could reconnect without the weight of their missions pressing down on them. For the first time in years, they were gathering not as strategists or warriors but as friends.

Maya arrived first, feeling an odd sense of nostalgia as she waited in the quiet mountain air. Soon, she heard the crunch of footsteps as Jules and Henri approached, both smiling as they embraced her.

"It's been too long," Jules said, her eyes bright with warmth.

Henri nodded. "Feels like we're stepping back in time. We started all this together, and here we are—still here, still fighting."

Shortly after, Raven and Dr. Moreno arrived, completing the circle. They gathered around a fire, sharing memories, stories, and laughter. For a moment, it felt as if the years had melted away, and they were once again the young, idealistic team who had dared to confront the impossible.

The Message of Continuity

As the evening deepened, the conversation turned to The Nexus's legacy and the impact it had achieved. Jules spoke of the journalists she now trained, young reporters who saw themselves as guardians of truth. Henri recounted the legal reforms that had been inspired by The Nexus's work, laws designed to protect whistleblowers and dismantle corruption. Raven, ever pragmatic, described her ongoing mentorship of activists, teaching them how to protect themselves in a world where power constantly shifted.

Finally, Maya spoke, her voice soft but resolute. "We've done something remarkable, but our work is not truly finished. The mission of The Nexus will outlive us, but we need to ensure that its heart remains true."

Dr. Moreno nodded thoughtfully. "We started with a vision, a purpose. But as it grows, The Nexus will need guidance, a touchstone to remind it of why it began."

They spent the next few days crafting a manifesto of sorts—a document that outlined the principles of The Nexus, a guide for future generations. They called it The Lightkeeper's Charter. It wasn't a set of rules or rigid protocols; it was a reminder of the spirit, the integrity, and the resilience that had guided them from the beginning.

The charter included the following pillars:

Integrity Over Influence: The Nexus would never seek power for power's sake. Its influence would only serve to protect truth and uphold justice.

Transparency and Accountability: Every action taken would be transparent to its members, ensuring that The Nexus remained a servant of the people, never a hidden force.

Empowerment of Communities: The Nexus was not just an organization but a movement. Its goal was to empower communities to fight for justice and hold power accountable in their own way.

Adapting Without Compromising Values: As threats and technologies evolved, The Nexus would adapt but never compromise its core principles. Each new challenge would be met with creativity, resilience, and an unwavering commitment to truth.

A Legacy of Courage: Above all, The Nexus would be a legacy of courage. Every member would be reminded that they were part of a lineage of people who dared to confront corruption, to protect the vulnerable, and to defend justice at any cost.

They signed the charter together, each understanding the gravity of what they were entrusting to the future. This document would be passed on, a reminder of the unity and vision that had brought The Nexus to life.

A New Beginning

Before they parted ways, Maya called for one final gathering. Standing together on a quiet mountainside, overlooking a vast expanse of snow-covered peaks, she looked at each of her friends, her voice filled with emotion.

"We've done something extraordinary," she said. "But we must accept that this is no longer ours to lead. We are passing the torch so that The Nexus can continue to shine, stronger than ever."

Jules placed a hand on her shoulder, her expression proud. "This is what we fought for—a legacy that will continue without us."

Henri nodded; his gaze distant but resolute. "It's time for the next generation to take up the fight, with fresh ideas, new strength, and the same commitment we held dear."

They shared quite goodbyes, each knowing this may be the last time they gathered in this way yet finding solace in the knowledge that their work would endure.

The Torch Passed

After returning from the retreat, Maya spent the following weeks preparing a select group of emerging leaders for a formal transition. She shared with them The Lightkeeper's Charter, her experiences, her mistakes, and her hopes. These young leaders were ready, eager to bring their own perspectives and innovations to The Nexus.

On the day of the official transition, Maya addressed The Nexus for the final time, speaking to members gathered across the globe through a secure broadcast.

"We started as a few voices, but now we are millions," she began, her voice steady and filled with pride. "The Nexus is no longer bound by any one leader or location. It is a movement, a promise, a symbol of resilience. And now, it belongs to you."

The broadcast ended, and as Maya stepped away, she felt a weight lift from her shoulders. The mission she had dedicated her life to was now in the hands of those ready to carry it forward. She had given everything, and now she had entrusted it to others who would breathe new life into The Nexus.

A Quiet Legacy

Maya retired to a small coastal town, where she continued to write, documenting her journey, the evolution of The Nexus, and the lessons she had learned along the way. Her writing became widely read, inspiring countless individuals who had never known her personally but felt connected to her mission.

And as she watched from afar, she saw The Nexus continue to grow, adapting, evolving, and inspiring change across the world. Communities around the globe used the tools, the courage, and the philosophy of The Nexus to protect their rights and their voices.

Maya knew that, though she had stepped back, her impact would remain. She had built a foundation of truth, justice, and courage—a legacy that would endure if people believed in the power of light to pierce the darkness.

The world was changing, and Maya's work had left an indelible mark. She had passed the torch, and in the hands of new leaders, The Nexus would continue its mission, as powerful and unstoppable as ever.

For Lily. For The Archivist. For everyone who had stood with her.

The light would never go out.

26

The Ripples of Influence

Years passed quietly for Maya in her coastal town. She watched The Nexus evolve from a distance, now a fully independent force that had woven itself into the fabric of societies worldwide. Its impact was undeniable, touching countless lives and reshaping the norms of accountability and transparency. Yet, even in her quiet life, Maya sensed the occasional tremors that the struggle between truth and power was ongoing.

One morning, as she walked along the shoreline, Maya received a message from an unexpected source. It was from Kira, one of the young leaders she had mentored during the transition, now a prominent figure within The Nexus. The message was brief, but its words stirred something deep within her:

"Maya, we've encountered something...unprecedented. We could use your guidance."

Though Maya had passed the torch, her sense of responsibility had never waned. She felt the old resolve awaken as she read Kira's message, her mind racing with the possibilities of what The Nexus might be facing.

A Return to the Front

Later that day, Maya joined a secure video call with Kira and several other Nexus leaders. Their expressions were serious, tempered with both urgency and respect for the woman who had started it all.

"We didn't want to disturb you," Kira began, her voice steady but edged with concern. "But we're dealing with a series of coordinated attacks that go beyond anything we've faced. It's as if The Collective—or whatever remains of it—has found a new strategy to undermine us."

Kira continued, describing how a network of disinformation campaigns, financial sabotage, and high-level infiltration had begun targeting Nexus cells around the globe. The attacks were sophisticated, carefully timed, and difficult to trace—an indication of a well-organized opposition that had evolved from the remnants of The Collective.

"We suspect they're working with new players," Kira said, her voice steady but laced with urgency. "Financial tech firms, rogue intelligence contractors, and even some political entities we've never seen involved before. It's almost as if they've formed a new syndicate, something more elusive and adaptable."

Maya listened intently, her mind processing the implications. This was different from the battles she had fought—an enemy that had adapted to The Nexus's tactics, one that was just as decentralized, just as covert. It was a network built in response to her creation, a counterbalance determined to resist the light she had brought.

"They're trying to break our foundation," Kira said. "But we're stronger than they realize. We just need to know how to adapt—how to stay a step ahead of them."

Maya felt a surge of pride. Kira's determination reminded her of her younger self, of the fire that had driven her through every hardship. She had passed the torch to capable hands, but now, perhaps, she could offer them a bit of wisdom.

"Thank you for reaching out," Maya replied, her voice calm and encouraging. "I may not have all the answers, but together, we can come up with a strategy. Remember: just as they adapt, so must we. And we have an advantage—they're reacting to our legacy, while we're building something that endures."

Strategizing a New Defense

Over the next few days, Maya worked closely with The Nexus leadership, offering guidance as they crafted a counterstrategy. They identified three key approaches to combat this new adversary: resilience, counterintelligence, and public mobilization.

Resilience: Maya advised them to further decentralize The Nexus's structure. Each cell would become even more self-reliant, developing its own local alliances and resources. This way, even if one part of The Nexus was compromised, the others could continue their work uninterrupted. They implemented training programs to strengthen the resilience of each cell, teaching members how to identify, resist, and counter attacks.

Counterintelligence: Working with Raven, who had continued her work in cyber strategy, they developed new encryption protocols and counter-surveillance techniques. They built a small but elite team within The

Nexus devoted entirely to identifying infiltrators, understanding the tactics of this new syndicate, and using predictive analytics to anticipate and thwart future attacks.

Public Mobilization: Maya suggested harnessing the support of the public as a shield against attacks. By increasing transparency and openly sharing their mission, The Nexus would make it harder for their enemies to discredit them. Public outreach campaigns were launched, inviting communities to participate in local Nexus initiatives, making The Nexus's impact more tangible and harder to dismiss as a faceless entity.

As Maya worked with the team, she felt a renewed sense of purpose. Her role had shifted, but she was still part of something larger, guiding the next generation as they faced the new challenges her own journey had inspired.

An Unexpected Encounter

One evening, after a long day of planning and strategizing, Maya received another message—this time from an encrypted source. The signature was familiar, sparking a wave of memories. It was Kaido.

"Maya, I've been following your progress. You're facing a formidable foe—one that sees you as an existential threat. But there's something you need to know. They have allies you wouldn't expect. We need to meet. This will be our last conversation."

The message was unsettling. Kaido, ever the ghost, had never contacted her without purpose. If he was reaching out now, it meant something profound was at stake. She arranged a meeting with him in a neutral location, taking every precaution to ensure security.

They met at a small café on the outskirts of a city, both disguised to avoid recognition. Kaido looked older, his face marked by years of secrecy and survival, yet his gaze was as sharp as ever.

"Maya," he began, his voice quieter, almost weary. "This new syndicate isn't just about power. They see The Nexus as a threat to the established order itself. Their goal is to discredit and dismantle it before it inspires further rebellion, before it becomes a model for something they can't control."

He handed her a file filled with names, dates, and locations—evidence of secret meetings between government officials, private intelligence firms, and leaders of multinational corporations, all of whom saw The Nexus as a disruptive force.

"They call themselves The Obsidian Alliance," he continued. "They operate under the guise of preserving stability, but their real purpose is to keep people compliant, to silence voices like yours before they ever gain traction."

Maya absorbed his words, feeling a deep sense of both urgency and understanding. The Obsidian Alliance was more than an enemy; it was a manifestation of the very forces she had been fighting all her life. She realized then that The Nexus's struggle would not end with one generation or even one lifetime. It was a movement that would have to evolve and adapt endlessly.

The New War Begins

Armed with Kaido's information, Maya and The Nexus prepared for a new phase of their mission. They no longer saw themselves as merely defenders of truth; they were now protectors of an ideal, a way of life that valued transparency, accountability, and courage over control and manipulation.

They launched a campaign called Operation Ember, designed to expose the workings of The Obsidian Alliance. The operation was multifaceted, involving everything from investigative journalism and whistleblower support to public education initiatives. They coordinated with international allies, NGOs, and independent media, creating a network of transparency that would make it nearly impossible for The Obsidian Alliance to operate without scrutiny.

As Operation Ember unfolded, The Nexus found themselves in a battle unlike any they had faced before. The Obsidian Alliance fought back with all its resources, deploying disinformation, legal maneuvers, and even intimidation tactics. But the more they fought, the more they revealed their true nature to the public. The Nexus's message grew stronger, resonating with people who were tired of living under invisible hands that dictated their lives without accountability.

The Ripple of Change

Months into Operation Ember, The Nexus achieved a significant breakthrough. Through careful infiltration, they managed to secure files linking The Obsidian Alliance to major policy manipulations, environmental abuses, and human rights violations worldwide. The evidence was released to the public, sparking outrage and demanding action from international authorities.

The public reaction was overwhelming. Protests erupted in major cities, and political leaders who had aligned themselves with The Obsidian Alliance faced mounting pressure to step down. The Obsidian Alliance found itself backed into a corner, exposed in a way it had never been before.

Maya watched with quiet pride as The Nexus stood at the center of this change, knowing that they were no longer simply exposing corruption but actively reshaping the world's understanding of power and transparency.

A Legacy Set in Motion

As The Nexus grew stronger, Maya knew her involvement was coming to a natural close. She had passed on everything she could, equipped the next generation with the tools, wisdom, and resilience needed to carry on the mission. She knew now that The Nexus was unstoppable—not because of any one person but because it belonged to the people, to every individual who had ever fought for the truth.

On her last day as an active advisor, Maya addressed The Nexus one final time, her voice steady and filled with quiet resolve.

"We've faced forces that tried to silence us, bend us, break us," she said. "But every time, we stood together, refusing to yield. The Nexus is more than an organization. It's an idea, an unbreakable promise that truth will always find a way."

After the call ended, Maya looked out at the horizon, the weight of years of struggle, sacrifice, and triumph settling over her like a gentle tide. She had done what she set out to do and more, shaping a movement that would endure long after her footsteps faded.

For Lily. For The Archivist. For everyone who had dared to stand with her.

The world was in their hands now, and she felt a profound peace in knowing that the future was brightened by the light she had helped ignite.

The torch was passed. The legacy continued. And The Nexus would live on, a beacon of resilience, courage, and hope for generations to come.

27

The New Dawn

Months passed quietly for Maya, as she watched from afar the ripples of her life's work unfold in ways she'd only dreamed. The Nexus was no longer an isolated movement; it had become a global phenomenon, inspiring initiatives in education, government, and independent media to prioritize transparency, accountability, and the courage to question authority.

Despite stepping back, Maya kept a pulse on The Nexus's journey. She maintained a respectable distance, knowing that the current leaders needed space to carve out their own vision. But one day, she received a message from Kira, the young leader she had once mentored. It was simple, just three words, but it carried a sense of urgency and a weight she recognized:

"We need you."

Return to the Field

Though she had sworn to leave the front lines, Maya knew she couldn't ignore the call. The message hinted at something critical, and she trusted Kira's judgment. Arriving at one of The Nexus's secure facilities, she was greeted by familiar faces—Kira, Raven, and Henri, now an advisor himself.

Kira's expression was serious, her usual confidence tempered by the gravity of the situation.

"Thank you for coming, Maya," she said, her voice steady. "We wouldn't have reached out if it wasn't urgent."

Kira led Maya and the others to a secure briefing room, where she pulled up an intelligence report on a screen. "We've recently intercepted communications from a group we hadn't seen before, one that calls itself The Anvil. It's a highly secretive, international consortium of private security firms, ex-military contractors, and high-level politicians."

Kira paused, her expression darkening. "They view The Nexus as a direct threat to their interests, and they're planning a full-scale assault—digital, financial, and, potentially, physical. Their goal is to dismantle us, cell by cell."

Maya studied intelligence with a sinking feeling. The Anvil was more than a rogue faction or a splinter group; it was a coalition of the powerful, those who profited from a world where accountability was scarce and secrecy abundant.

"We've faced retaliation before," Maya said slowly. "But this... this is a declaration of war."

Operation Shield: Preparing for the Attack

The Nexus was no stranger to threats, but The Anvil's sophistication required a new level of readiness. Maya and Kira devised Operation Shield; a multi-layered defensive strategy designed to protect The Nexus's cells worldwide. Operation Shield had three main components:

Digital Fortification: Raven led the effort to reinforce cybersecurity across all Nexus networks. She collaborated with white-hat hackers and cybersecurity experts, implementing advanced encryption and self-sustaining data systems that would render each Nexus cell practically invisible online.

Counter-Intelligence and Surveillance: Henri and his team developed a counter-surveillance initiative, using predictive analysis to anticipate The Anvil's movements. They tracked key Anvil operatives, gathering intelligence on their methods and vulnerabilities, ensuring that The Nexus could respond in real time to any sudden threats.

Community Resilience: Understanding that The Anvil might attempt to sway public opinion, Kira organized a global outreach initiative to strengthen The Nexus's grassroots support. Through workshops, public forums, and educational programs, they empowered communities to stand with The Nexus, creating a protective layer of public solidarity.

Maya observed each phase of Operation Shield with a mix of pride and resolve. The new leaders had risen to the occasion with resilience and precision, ready to defend what they had built. She realized her role was not to lead but to lend her knowledge and experience, to guide them through the darkness as they had once guided her.

The Anvil's First Strike

Not long after Operation Shield was deployed, The Anvil launched its first attack. It began with a series of cyber assaults aimed at Nexus servers, attempting to breach security protocols and access sensitive information. But thanks to Raven's fortifications, the attacks were thwarted at every turn.

Frustrated by the digital defenses, The Anvil moved to more overt tactics, attempting to discredit The Nexus in the media. They spread rumors, falsified documents, and planted stories accusing The Nexus of everything from espionage to inciting civil unrest. News outlets began publishing articles questioning the organization's motives, causing a wave of doubt that threatened to undermine The Nexus's credibility.

Kira quickly responded, rallying the network's public relations team to refute the claims with transparency and evidence. In a bold move, she held a live broadcast where she directly addressed the allegations, calling out The Anvil's tactics and reaffirming The Nexus's commitment to justice and accountability. Her words resonated with supporters worldwide, sparking a renewed wave of public support.

The Anvil had underestimated The Nexus's ability to rally its allies. The attempted smear campaign backfired, and public sympathy shifted even more decisively toward The Nexus. Still, Maya knew that The Anvil would not be easily deterred. Their strength lay in persistence, and they would likely resort to more direct measures.

The Underground Network

With each failed assault, The Anvil's tactics grew more desperate. Intercepted communications revealed that they were preparing for a coordinated, physical strike against Nexus hubs. This posed an unprecedented risk; while The Nexus had faced individual threats before, they had never confronted an organized, militarized assault.

In response, Maya proposed a bold plan: The Underground Network. Drawing on her years of experience, she suggested that The Nexus cells temporarily go dark, shifting to hidden locations, operating only through secure channels, and building a network of decoys that would lead The Anvil's operatives away from their true bases.

Kira was hesitant. "Won't this make it look like we're retreating? People might think we're giving up."

Maya shook her head. "Sometimes, the best defense is to disappear, to become the ghost they can't catch. The Underground Network will buy us time, allow us to regroup and assess The Anvil's strategies. And once we're ready, we'll resurface stronger than ever."

The Nexus cells went dark, dispersing into secure locations around the world, each cell operating independently, yet all connected by encrypted communication lines. They created decoy hubs, leaving false trails and misleading information that sent The Anvil on a wild chase through cities and rural areas alike.

The Anvil's forces, frustrated and exhausted, found themselves chasing shadows, wasting resources and exposing their methods in the process. With each misstep, The Nexus gathered more intelligence, mapping The Anvil's hierarchy, resources, and internal conflicts.

A Strategic Counteroffensive

As the Underground Network took shape, The Nexus prepared for a strategic counteroffensive. They identified weak points within The Anvil's structure—rivalries between key leaders, financial vulnerabilities, and dependency on third-party contractors.

Working with Kira and Raven, Maya developed a plan to exploit these weaknesses. They launched Operation Mirage, a series of covert actions designed to destabilize The Anvil from within:

Financial Sabotage: By exposing The Anvil's illicit financial dealings, The Nexus triggered investigations by international regulatory bodies. Frozen accounts and seized assets weakened The Anvil's funding, limiting their ability to maintain operations.

Disinformation Campaign: The Nexus used The Anvil's own tactics against them, planting information that suggested dissent among their ranks. As paranoia and mistrust spread, The Anvil's leadership struggled to maintain unity, causing fractures that weakened their efforts.

Targeted Exposés: The Nexus released a series of detailed reports exposing The Anvil's ties to corrupt officials, illegal arms trades, and human rights abuses. These reports gained global attention, tarnishing The Anvil's reputation and causing their public support to collapse.

The Anvil, once a formidable opponent, began to unravel. The very tactics they had used to control and manipulate were now turned against them, eroding their influence and weakening their ability to operate in secrecy.

A Victory for The Nexus

After months of relentless counteroffensives, The Anvil's coalition disintegrated. Its leaders, stripped of resources and public support, went into hiding, while some attempted to negotiate leniency by testifying against their former allies. The Nexus's resilience had triumphed, proving once again that no force could silence the truth for long.

In a final public statement, Kira addressed The Nexus's supporters worldwide, acknowledging the sacrifice and courage that had brought them through the struggle.

"This victory belongs to all of us," she said, her voice filled with pride. "We have shown that truth cannot be hidden, that justice cannot be bought, and that no force on earth can silence a movement fueled by integrity. We are The Nexus, and our mission endures."

Maya watched Kira's speech from her quiet retreat, a deep sense of fulfillment settling over her. She knew now, beyond any doubt, that The Nexus was in capable hands. Her role was complete, and her legacy was safe.

The Legacy of Light

In the following years, The Nexus continued to grow, inspiring new generations to fight for transparency and accountability. Governments around the world began adopting policies modeled after The Nexus's ideals, creating a ripple effect of integrity and resilience across societies.

Maya, though she had returned to a quiet life, remained a guiding figure. Her writings, reflections, and strategic insights became essential readings for young leaders, a testament to the journey that had led to this new era of truth and justice.

And as she walked along the shoreline one evening, watching the sunset cast a warm glow over the water, Maya felt a profound peace. She had passed the torch, created a legacy that would outlive her, and seen her life's work become a force for change.

The Nexus, now a symbol of light in a world that once thrived on shadows, would endure. For Lily. For The Archivist. For everyone who had joined her in the pursuit of a world built on courage and truth.

The light would continue, carried forward by countless voices, unstoppable and unyielding.

And if there were those willing to stand, to speak, and to fight, the legacy of The Nexus would remain—a beacon of hope in a world forever transformed.

28

A New Frontier

Years passed, and Maya's legacy continued to ripple through The Nexus and beyond. She had lived quietly, content with the knowledge that her life's work had become a living, breathing force. But one evening, as she sat by the fireplace, she received a message that hinted at an emerging threat—something that could potentially undo much of what The Nexus had achieved.

The message was from an anonymous sender, the words urgent yet cryptic:

"They're watching, waiting. There's a new order forming—a convergence of technology and control. If The Nexus isn't prepared, everything we've fought for could be erased. Look to the new frontier."

Maya's heart quickened. She knew that technology had always been a double-edged sword tool for both liberation and control. But this message suggested a more advanced threat, something that transcended mere power plays and alliances. She had to know more.

The Digital Dominion

Reaching out to Kira and Raven, Maya requested a secure briefing to share her concerns. Within days, she was back in a Nexus facility, meeting with the core team she had entrusted years before. The world was now during a technological revolution: AI advancements, biometric surveillance, and data mining had reached unprecedented levels. Governments, corporations, and powerful individuals had the ability to manipulate digital landscapes and, by extension, influence public perception and behavior on a mass scale.

Raven took the floor, presenting what she had uncovered through The Nexus's cyber intelligence team. "There's a new network forming in the shadows, Maya. We're calling them The Digital Dominion. They're a coalition of tech giants, biotech firms, and AI conglomerates with access to more data than any one organization has ever held. Their goal is not just to influence it's control over information itself. They want to shape reality as people perceive it."

She paused, a troubled look on her face. "They're developing technology that can create convincing deepfakes, alter digital records, and even influence people's behavior through subtle algorithms. If they succeed, they could rewrite history in real-time, erase truths, and manufacture consensus."

Maya felt a chill. This was a frontier she had foreseen but never anticipated arriving so soon. The Nexus had been prepared to fight shadowy alliances and corrupt systems, but this new threat was different. The Digital Dominion could control information on a fundamental level, turning truth into a variable they could manipulate at will.

"We need to understand their methods, their reach, and their weaknesses," Maya said, her voice steady. "The Nexus was built to protect truth, and we will adapt to defend it—even in a world where reality can be digitally altered."

The Sentinel Project

The team knew that combating The Digital Dominion would require new strategies, resources, and allies. Together, they developed The Sentinel Project, an initiative designed to counter the manipulation of information at its source. The project had three core components:

Decentralized Data Verification: Raven led the creation of a blockchain-based verification system, ensuring that any piece of data could be traced back to its origin. This system would use cryptographic proofs to validate information, making it impossible for The Digital Dominion to alter records without detection.

Public Awareness Campaigns: Kira launched an international campaign to educate people about digital manipulation, deepfakes, and algorithmic control. By raising awareness, they hoped to create a more informed public that could resist subtle forms of influence. The campaign focused on digital literacy, critical thinking, and the tools people could use to verify information.

Independent Data Hubs: Maya proposed a global network of independent data hubs—small, decentralized nodes that would serve as trusted repositories of verified information. These hubs would be community-run, accessible to anyone, and insulated from centralized control. The hubs could distribute truth globally, making it difficult for The Digital Dominion to suppress or alter facts.

Maya knew this was an ambitious plan, perhaps the most challenging project The Nexus had ever undertaken. But she also knew it was necessary. If The Nexus could create a system that upheld the integrity of information, they could protect future generations from the dangers of an entirely manufactured reality.

Building Alliances on the New Frontier

Understanding the magnitude of The Sentinel Project, The Nexus reached out to technologists, digital rights activists, and AI ethicists. They formed alliances with organizations focused on digital transparency, cybersecurity, and open-source technology. By uniting these forces, The Nexus aimed to create a coalition dedicated to defending the digital world from manipulation and control.

One of the most influential allies they secured was Dr. Elias Tanaka, a renowned AI researcher who had once worked for a corporation now aligned with The Digital Dominion. Disillusioned his work had been used, Dr. Tanaka agreed to help The Nexus, offering his expertise in AI ethics and algorithmic transparency.

Dr. Tanaka worked closely with Raven and Kira, designing tools that could detect and expose manipulative algorithms. Together, they developed a real-time tracking system that analyzed digital platforms for bias, influence, and covert manipulation, providing users with insight into how content was being tailored to sway their perception.

Maya watched the alliance grow, feeling a renewed sense of hope. This was a new battlefield, but they were not alone. With every expert who joined, with every individual who believed in The Nexus's mission, she saw the foundation of something unbreakable—an internet, and perhaps a world, protected by those who valued truth above all else.

The Battle for Digital Sovereignty

As The Sentinel Project gained traction, The Digital Dominion took notice. The Nexus began facing a new wave of attacks: attempts to hack the independent data hubs, coordinated disinformation campaigns targeting their allies, and even legal action intended to cripple their operations. The Digital Dominion had deep resources, including law firms, cybersecurity mercenaries, and media influence.

Maya and her team, however, were undeterred. They had anticipated these challenges, and The Sentinel Project had been built to withstand attacks. The decentralized nature of the data hubs made it nearly impossible to infiltrate on a large scale, and the blockchain-based verification system held strong, maintaining the integrity of the information.

In response to The Digital Dominion's legal maneuvers, The Nexus engaged in a public campaign to expose the Dominion's tactics. They published a series of exposés detailing the ways in which The Digital Dominion attempted to manipulate legal and media systems to maintain control. Public awareness grew, and governments around the world were pressured to enact digital rights laws that protected citizens from invasive algorithms and data exploitation.

The Digital Dominion's grip began to weaken as The Nexus and its allies stood their ground, pushing for transparency, accountability, and the right to an unaltered reality.

The Turning Point

The conflict reached a climax when The Digital Dominion attempted one final, audacious move: they launched a system-wide hack targeting The Nexus's data hubs, aiming to destroy The Sentinel Project's infrastructure. This was a last-ditch effort to destabilize The Nexus and end its influence once and for all.

But The Nexus was prepared. Raven and her cybersecurity team had anticipated such a move, and they countered with a sophisticated defense protocol that redirected the attack, exposing The Dominion's own systems to public scrutiny. In a matter of hours, the hack was traced back to The Dominion, and their efforts to control information were exposed on a global scale.

With public outrage at a peak, international investigations were launched into The Digital Dominion's activities. Lawsuits, sanctions, and public outcry dismantled their operations, and many of their high-ranking members faced prosecution.

The Nexus had won. But Maya knew that this was a victory in an ongoing struggle. The world of technology and power was ever-changing, and the next threat would undoubtedly arise in new forms. However, The Sentinel Project remained a beacon of hope, a promise that The Nexus would protect the truth, no matter how complex the battlefield became.

A Legacy Redefined

In the aftermath, Maya gathered The Nexus's core team one last time. The world was changing, and she wanted them to understand the legacy they were building.

"We've safeguarded truth," she said, her voice filled with pride. "But remember—this isn't just about protecting information. It's about ensuring that people can live in a world where they know what's real, where their choices aren't dictated by those who profit from deception."

Kira stepped forward; her expression thoughtful. "The Sentinel Project is more than a defense. It's a foundation. We've created something that allows people to reclaim their voices, to own their reality. It's something that will grow beyond us."

Maya nodded, a profound sense of fulfillment settling over her. "Exactly. And as long as we hold to that, The Nexus will remain unbreakable."

As the meeting concluded, Maya felt the quiet satisfaction of a journey complete. She had led The Nexus from its inception, through challenges, victories, and evolutions she'd never imagined. And now, she saw that her life's work was in good hands, stronger than it had ever been.

The Sentinel of Truth

Years later, The Sentinel Project became a cornerstone of digital culture worldwide. Its principles influenced educational systems, technology policies, and even corporate ethics. People learned to question what they saw, to verify information, and to trust in their ability to discern truth from illusion. The Nexus was no longer just an organization; it was a global movement, a symbol of resilience in an era of uncertainty.

And Maya, quietly retired but forever vigilant, knew that the light would continue.

For Lily. For The Archivist. For everyone who had dared to believe in the power of truth.

The Nexus—and the Sentinel Project—were here to stay, guardians of a future where reality could no longer be manipulated by a few. A world redefined by courage, built on a foundation of integrity, and illuminated by the unwavering light of truth.

29

Return to Echo Park

After years away, Maya felt a quiet tug leading her back to Los Angeles. Echo Park, once the place where she'd found her purpose, was calling to her again. She had walked those streets as a young woman, filled with the fire of ambition and the resolve to change the world. Now, with her life's work woven into the fabric of society, she felt drawn to the place where it had all begun.

Maya wasn't certain what she was looking for in Echo Park, but she knew it was something she needed to see for herself—perhaps to find a sense of closure, or maybe just to reconnect with the roots of her journey.

A Familiar Landscape

Arriving at Echo Park, Maya took in the landscape. The city had changed; there were new buildings, new faces, but the essence of the place felt the same. The lake shimmered in the afternoon sun, and people moved along the walking paths, laughing and talking, unaware of the quiet revolution she had ignited here so many years ago.

Maya walked slowly, taking in every detail—the park benches, the smell of food from nearby vendors, the sound of laughter and music in the distance. She felt a deep sense of nostalgia, mixed with pride. This was where she had first realized the power of standing up, of refusing to accept the world as it was. And now, looking around, she saw a community more connected, more aware, and more resilient than it had ever been.

As she walked along the lake, Maya noticed a small gathering by the boathouse. Curious, she moved closer, and soon realized it was a community event, a public forum discussing local issues. The forum reminded her of The Nexus's early days, when she and her team had organized grassroots gatherings to educate and inspire the community.

Smiling to herself, she sat down on a nearby bench to watch, feeling a quiet satisfaction in seeing the spirit of The Nexus alive in the very place it had started.

An Unexpected Encounter

As the forum wrapped up, Maya turned to leave, but a familiar voice stopped her in her tracks. "I thought I recognized you."

She turned to see an older woman with kind eyes and a knowing smile—Lillian, a community leader who had once helped Maya organize those first meetings in Echo Park. They had worked together, building a foundation of trust and shared purpose that had inspired Maya's work with The Nexus.

Maya's face lit up. "Lillian! It's been so long."

They embraced, both moved by the unexpected reunion. Lillian looked at Maya, her gaze warm and appreciative. "You've come a long way. I always knew you'd make a difference, even back then."

They sat on the bench together, watching the sun begin to set over the lake. Lillian shared updates on the community, speaking of the changes and challenges that had shaped Echo Park over the years. Maya listened intently, feeling the years melt away as they reconnected.

"I've followed your work, you know," Lillian said, a proud smile on her face. "The Nexus is incredible. You've inspired people all over the world. But seeing you back here... I must wonder, what brings you back to Echo Park?"

Maya looked out over the lake, considering her answer. "I think... I needed to remember where it all started. To remind myself of the roots that grounded me. Sometimes it's easy to lose sight of things when you're caught up in the bigger picture."

Lillian nodded. "It's true. No matter how far you go, places like this are with you. Echo Park shaped you as much as you shaped it."

They sat in comfortable silence, the weight of shared memories between them. Maya felt a deep sense of peace, realizing that Echo Park wasn't just a place from her past—it was part of her foundation, a reminder of why she had fought so hard and sacrificed so much.

A Passing of the Torch

As they continued to talk, a young woman approached them. She held a notepad and a pen, bright eyes with curiosity. She introduced herself as Emily, a local journalist who had been covering the forum and noticed Maya and Lillian sitting together.

"I've read about The Nexus," Emily said, her voice filled with admiration. "You've done so much. I've been trying to do my part, reporting on issues that matter. But sometimes it feels... overwhelming."

Maya smiled, seeing a reflection of her younger self in the young journalist's eyes. She gestured for Emily to sit with them. "It can be overwhelming," Maya admitted, "but you don't have to do it all at once. Start with what you can change right here, in your own community. Sometimes the most meaningful impact begins on a small scale."

Emily listened, captivated, and soon the conversation shifted to stories of the past, of the early days in Echo Park when Maya had first found her voice, and the long journey she had taken since. She shared lessons she had learned, the value of persistence, and the importance of never underestimating the power of a single person to inspire change.

As the evening grew darker, Emily thanked them both, her determination reignited. "Thank you, Maya. I'll keep working, and I'll remember what you've told me. Echo Park still has a lot of stories that need to be told."

Lillian smiled as Emily walked away. "And so it goes. Another generation, ready to pick up the torch."

Maya nodded, feeling a profound sense of fulfillment. "Yes. And that's exactly how it should be."

Full Circle

As Maya prepared to leave, she walked to the edge of the lake, looking out over the water as the city lights began to reflect on its surface. She took a deep breath, feeling the familiar weight of Echo Park settle over her. This place had shaped her, given her purpose, and now she could see it was ready to nurture a new generation.

She knew that her role in The Nexus was complete. The mission, the legacy, and the impact she had dreamed of had come full circle. Her work would continue, carried on by those who had been inspired by her journey, each one leaving their own mark on the world.

As she stood there, she felt a gentle sense of closure, a final connection with the place that had been both her beginning and her foundation.

The Legacy Lives On

Maya left Echo Park that night with a heart full of peace and gratitude. She knew she wouldn't be returning; the torch had passed, and a new generation was ready to take the lead. The Nexus would continue, an unbreakable chain of resilience and courage.

In her quiet, final days, Maya often reflected on the ripples her life had created. She knew that wherever truth was defended, wherever people stood up for justice, and wherever voices refused to be silenced, a piece of Echo Park would live on.

And that was enough.

For Lily. For The Archivist. For everyone who had joined her along the way.

The legacy of The Nexus—and the spirit of Echo Park—would live on, a beacon of hope in a world that had been forever changed.

30

Whispers in the Dark

Back in her quiet coastal home, Maya embraced the peaceful rhythm of retirement. She had made her final return to Echo Park, where her journey had begun, and said farewell to The Nexus. But even now, the habits of a lifetime are hard to shake. She kept herself informed, tracking The Nexus's activities from a distance, her ear still attuned to the subtle shifts and currents that signaled change in the world.

One evening, as she sifted through news reports, a strange email appeared in her inbox. The sender was unlisted, and the subject line read only: FOR YOUR EYES ONLY. Maya's heart quickened. Messages like this rarely came without purpose.

She opened it cautiously. The text was brief and cryptic, only a single line, but it was enough to catch her attention:

"They have found the Archivist's notes. They know what he left behind."

Maya froze. The Archivist—a codename they had only spoken of in whispers—was a long-lost ally, a brilliant but elusive figure who had once worked deep within The Nexus, gathering intelligence and information on corruption at the highest levels. Before he'd vanished, he'd compiled secrets so dangerous that The Nexus had agreed to seal them away, hidden from even its own members. His notes were rumored to contain information that could destabilize governments, expose new players, and illuminate networks they hadn't even known existed.

But the Archivist had been gone for years, presumed lost.

Her hand trembled slightly as she scrolled down. Beneath the message was a set of coordinates, pinpointing a location in an unassuming mountain region outside of Zurich, Switzerland. A second line followed, equally enigmatic:

"Meet me where the river splits. Midnight."

Maya's mind raced. Who was the message from? How could anyone has located the Archivist's notes? And what secrets were hidden in those documents that could possibly be so dangerous even now? She knew that The Nexus's new leaders, capable though they were, were unaware of the Archivist's existence. She hadn't told them. She hadn't told anyone. Those secrets were buried with the past.

But now, the past was reaching out, calling her back into the shadows.

A Journey into the Unknown

By midnight the next day, Maya had boarded a flight to Zurich. She moved discreetly, keeping a low profile. She arrived in the mountain region near the coordinates, the air crisp and silent as she made her way through the unfamiliar terrain. Following the directions in the message, she found herself at the bank of a quiet river that wound through the mountain valley. Here, where the river forked into two narrow streams, she waited.

The forest around her was hushed, the night stretching long and heavy. Shadows danced under the trees, and the only sound was the gentle rush of water. Maya checked her watch: it was exactly midnight.

A figure emerged from the darkness, their steps silent and sure. The person wore a hood, their face obscured, but Maya recognized the slight limp, the careful gait. Her breath caught. It couldn't be.

The figure pulled back the hood, revealing an older man with intense eyes and a familiar, somber expression.

"Maya," he said, his voice carrying a trace of disbelief. "I didn't think you'd come."

She felt a surge of emotions—shock, relief, suspicion—all tangled together. "Archivist... how?"

He gave a weary smile. "That's a story for another time. Right now, we have more pressing matters. I'm not the only one who's after these notes."

Her pulse quickened. "What's going on? I thought you'd... I thought you'd disappeared for good."

The Archivist looked down; his face shadowed. "I had to vanish. The information I gathered... it was too volatile. It threatened people I cared about. I had to protect them, so I made sure no one could follow my trail."

He reached into his coat and pulled out a weathered notebook, placing it gently into her hands. "But something's changed. There's a new player. I don't know who they are, but they've been looking for me—and for this."

Maya opened the notebook, flipping through the pages. She saw names, diagrams, and maps that revealed hidden networks and alliances she'd never seen before. This wasn't just intelligence; it was a blueprint of unseen power structures, new forces she hadn't known existed.

As she turned to the last page, she noticed a single word scrawled in the Archivist's hurried handwriting: Equinox.

"What does it mean?" she asked, looking up.

The Archivist's face darkened. "I don't know yet. But I suspect it's connected to a much larger operation, something that's been in motion for years. Equinox isn't just a codeword. It's an event. A convergence."

A chill ran through Maya. "And what happens when Equinox arrives?"

He shook his head. "That's what I've been trying to find out. But there's a group—powerful, hidden. They call themselves The Veritas Collective. They know about Equinox, and they believe it will allow them to control not just information, but reality itself. If they succeed, everything we've built with The Nexus could be erased overnight."

The silence between them grew heavy as Maya absorbed the weight of his words. The Veritas Collective. The name alone suggested a group that believed in shaping truth on a fundamental level, bending perception, and controlling the narrative of history itself.

She took a steady breath. "Then we need to find them, stop them before this... Equinox happens."

The Archivist's eyes were grave. "Yes. But there's one more thing you should know. Equinox... it's already in motion. We don't have much time."

A Shadow on the Horizon

As dawn broke over the mountains, Maya and the Archivist parted ways, each taking separate routes to avoid detection. They had agreed to reconvene in Zurich, where they would plan their next steps. Maya knew she would have to bring Kira and the rest of The Nexus back into the fold—this threat was too great for her to face alone.

But as she walked along the river, her mind raced with questions. How long had this Veritas Collective existed? How far did their influence reach? And what did Equinox truly entail?

Suddenly, her phone vibrated. She pulled it from her pocket, glancing down at an unknown number that had sent a single message.

"Maya, you're getting close. Stop now or face the consequences."

She stared at the screen, a sense of dread creeping over her. Whoever had sent the message knew she was here, knew what she was searching for. The Veritas Collective had eyes everywhere.

And she realized, with a cold certainty, that this was only the beginning. Equinox was coming. The Veritas Collective was waiting.

And Maya was about to walk into the deepest shadow she had ever known.

The stakes had never been higher. The final battle for reality itself had begun.

Epilogue

Shadows and Light

The months following her encounter with the Archivist were a whirlwind. Maya had rejoined The Nexus, rallying her allies to prepare for what was coming. The Veritas Collective and their ominous Equinox operation loomed as a shadow over everything they had built. It was no longer just about protecting information; it was about defending the very fabric of reality, the truth that kept society grounded.

From their headquarters in Zurich, Maya and her closest allies—Kira, Raven, and Henri—poured over the Archivist's notes, decrypting fragments of hidden connections, financial flows, and cryptic messages. The Veritas Collective, they discovered, wasn't merely a syndicate; it was a centuries-old organization dedicated to rewriting history and shaping global consciousness, a hand unseen but ever-present, guiding humanity toward an agenda known only to its shadowy leaders.

They found references to key individuals in politics, media, and science who were part of the Collective's network. Every piece of intelligence pointed to an event—a convergence of information, technology, and influence that would allow them to enact the Equinox. But what it truly meant was still a mystery.

One night, as Maya studied the last of the Archivist's notes, she discovered a new clue. Scribbled in a margin, she found the words: "Look to Echo."

Her breath caught. Echo Park—the place where her journey had begun, where she had first dreamed of creating The Nexus. Was this a coincidence, or did the Veritas Collective know something about her past?

She felt a deep chill as the pieces began to connect. Echo Park was more than a memory. It was part of the Collective's history too, a place where, years before she'd even realized it, their plans had intersected with her own. Somehow, the Collective had been aware of her all along.

A Return to the Beginning

Three weeks later, Maya returned to Echo Park, feeling the weight of her history there. She was alone this time, dressed inconspicuously as she moved through the familiar paths. The lake shimmered in the midday sun, families and friends enjoying a peaceful afternoon as if the world weren't on the brink of transformation.

Following the Archivist's notes, she found herself at an old, unmarked building on the edge of the park, a place she'd never noticed before. She slipped inside, descending a narrow stairwell that led into the basement, its walls covered in faded murals of revolutionaries and symbols of resistance.

In the dim light, she saw an unexpected sight: a library, its shelves filled with archives dating back over a century. These were records of resistance movements, uprisings, and social changes, a chapter in the battle against manipulation and control. At the center of the room stood a single desk, and on it, a sealed envelope bearing her name.

Maya approached, her hands trembling slightly as she broke the seal. Inside, she found a letter from the Archivist:

"Maya, if you're reading this, it means you've reached the beginning of the end. Echo Park is not only where you began; it is where they began, too. The Veritas Collective was here, long before you, hiding in plain sight. This library, these records—these are fragments of their history, buried in the shadows. You are the key to exposing it all. The Equinox will soon be upon us, and they will attempt to erase everything. But they cannot erase what is remembered."

At the bottom of the letter was a date: the next equinox.

She felt a surge of understanding and fear. The Veritas Collective planned to use the equinox—a symbolic balance of light and dark—as the moment to launch their final operation, one that would overwrite the past, control the present, and dictate the future. But she now held something they hadn't anticipated: their own history, preserved in the records surrounding her.

Maya realized her final task: she would reveal everything. She would expose the Collective's secrets, their origins, their methods, their agenda. She would bring them to light, destroying their power once and for all.

The Final Broadcast

In the weeks that followed, The Nexus worked tirelessly, digitizing every document, every record from the hidden library in Echo Park. On the day of the equinox, they prepared to release the data, broadcasting it worldwide in a public exposé that would reveal the truth about the Veritas Collective and their plans.

As the clock struck midnight, Maya initiated the broadcast. Across the world, people tuned in, watching as The Nexus unveiled the secrets of the Collective. The web of influence, the hidden agendas, the manipulation of history itself, every piece of their dark legacy was laid bare.

And as the broadcast continued, Maya delivered a final message:

"To those who seek to control reality, know this: truth is stronger than any shadow you can cast. We are The Nexus, and we are here to defend what is real, what is human, what is true."

For a moment, she felt an overwhelming peace. The truth was out. The people would see, would question, would reclaim their reality.

But as the broadcast ended, her phone vibrated. She looked down, and a single message appeared on the screen from an unknown number:

"This was only the beginning. Equinox is inevitable."

A chill ran down her spine as she realized that the Collective might have contingencies, plans she hadn't yet uncovered. The world was on the precipice of something unknown, and the next phase of the battle would be unlike anything she had ever faced.

The broadcast had brought The Nexus and the Veritas Collective into full view of one another, and now, the final showdown was looming.

And as Maya looked out over the city, she knew one thing for certain:

The fight was far from over.

Act I: Shadows in the Light

Chapter 1: The Aftermath of the Broadcast

After The Nexus's global broadcast, people around the world react to the revelations about the Veritas Collective. Some are shocked, others are skeptical, while governments and media outlets are thrown into chaos.

Maya and her team brace for retaliation from the Collective, suspecting that the group will move swiftly to maintain control over their agenda.

Kira and Raven work to protect key Nexus cells from inevitable counterattacks, while Maya reflects on her final mission with the organization.

Chapter 2: Equinox Unveiled

The Archivist re-emerges, warning Maya and her team that the Veritas Collective has accelerated its plans. He reveals that Equinox is not just an operation, but a coordinated event involving advanced AI, quantum computing, and mass psychological manipulation.

The Collective's goal is to create a "controlled reality," using Equinox as a psychological and technological event that influences millions simultaneously, rewriting beliefs, memories, and histories in a single, coordinated strike.

Maya realizes the extent of the threat: if Equinox succeeds, people's perceptions of the past and present could be permanently altered.

Chapter 3: The Nexus in Crisis

The Veritas Collective launches a series of coordinated cyber-attacks against The Nexus, disabling communication channels and disrupting resources.

Maya and her team go underground, relying on their most trusted allies to rebuild and secure their networks.

A message from an unknown source warns them that a mole within The Nexus is leaking information to the Collective. Suspicion grows, causing division and mistrust among the core members.

Act II: Into the Depths

Chapter 4: The Hunt for the Mole

Raven and Henri lead an investigation within The Nexus to uncover the mole, tracing communication logs and re-evaluating trusted allies.

As Maya coordinates from a hidden location, she reflects on her earlier days and her decision to keep the Archivist's notes hidden. She wonders if secrecy inadvertently endangered them all.

The mole is revealed to be a high-ranking Nexus member coerced into working for the Collective under threats to their family. The team removes them quietly, knowing the Collective's surveillance remains close.

Chapter 5: Allies in the Shadows

The Archivist introduces Maya to a former Veritas Collective member turned informant. This mysterious ally, known only as "Echo," provides insight into the Collective's tactics, revealing the role of high-ranking officials and tech companies.

Echo warns that Equinox's timeline is accelerating, with new phases set to begin in just days.

Maya and her team plan to intercept the Collective's communications, hoping to learn the final stage of Equinox. They also strategize a counter-broadcast to disrupt the event in real-time.

Chapter 6: The Final Countdown

As The Nexus decodes intercepted files, they discover that Equinox will involve a mass brainwave synchronization technology, coupled with a global digital feed. This will allow the Collective to transmit subtle changes in perception directly into the minds of millions.

Raven and Kira lead an operation to disrupt the synchronization points, knowing it's a high-risk mission that could expose them to capture.

Meanwhile, Maya receives a cryptic message from the Archivist indicating that there's a hidden layer within Equinox—something far more sinister and personal than they had realized.

Act III: The Revelation

Chapter 7: The Collective Strikes Back

The Veritas Collective discovers The Nexus's interference and begins a ruthless campaign to dismantle the organization. Nexus cells around the world report unprecedented attacks.

Maya and her core team narrowly escape an assassination attempt, leaving them with limited resources and a dwindling network.

In the chaos, Maya uncovers information that points to Echo Park as a crucial site in the final stage of Equinox, reinforcing the mysterious ties between her past and the Collective.

Chapter 8: A Return to Echo Park

Maya and her team return to Echo Park, following a series of clues that lead them to an underground facility built beneath the park. Here, they discover archives and equipment once used by the early founders of the Veritas Collective.

They find evidence that reveals the Collective's founder was a former friend and mentor of Maya's, someone who had believed in her early mission but ultimately turned to control rather than liberation.

Maya confronts her own history, realizing that her early ideals were co-opted by the Collective long before The Nexus was formed.

Chapter 9: The Truth About Equinox

In the hidden archives, they discover that Equinox's true purpose is to create a "synthetic reality," a virtual layer overlaid onto everyday life that subtly dictates behavior, suppressing critical thought and controlling population behavior on a mass scale.

Maya finds a hidden file addressed to her from the Archivist, explaining that the Collective had been working on Equinox for decades, refining its tools and tactics until they became practically invisible.

The Archivist warns that to stop Equinox, Maya must confront the founder of the Collective in person—a figure operating under the alias "Orion."

Act IV: Confrontation and Resolution

Chapter 10: The Battle Begins

The Nexus broadcasts the truth about Equinox to the world, but The Collective counters with disinformation, casting doubt on Maya's words and discrediting The Nexus.

Echo, the informant, contacts Maya with the location of Orion, the founder of the Veritas Collective, who is reportedly hiding in a fortified compound outside of Zurich.

Maya, Kira, Raven, and a select team of Nexus operatives prepare for a final showdown with Orion, hoping to disable Equinox's central control and prevent its activation.

Chapter 11: Face to Face with Orion

Maya and her team infiltrate Orion's compound, navigating a series of security traps and coming face to face with high-tech weaponry designed to protect Equinox's control center.

In a climactic confrontation, Maya finally meets Orion, who reveals their vision: a "perfect" society where information flows are controlled to prevent chaos and dissent.

Orion attempts to sway Maya, arguing that people are safer when reality is "guided," not left to chance and individual whims. But Maya, steadfast, argues that freedom and truth are worth the messiness of free will.

Chapter 12: The Destruction of Equinox

Maya and her team manage to destroy Equinox's central system, narrowly escaping as the facility collapses. Orion is captured but refuses to divulge the identities of other Collective members.

In one final, encrypted message from Orion, Maya receives a warning: "There will always be those who believe in control over chaos. Our cause will live on, in forms you cannot yet imagine."

Epilogue: The Legacy of The Nexus

Back in Echo Park, Maya reflects on her journey, the Collective, and the battle she and The Nexus have fought to protect truth.

She realizes that the fight for reality, for unfiltered truth, is a timeless struggle—one that will persist beyond her lifetime.

With a renewed sense of purpose, she prepares a final manifesto, passing it on to Kira and the new Nexus leaders, entrusting them with the mission to continue guarding the truth.

As she steps away, she feels both a sense of closure and the haunting knowledge that the Veritas Collective, in one form or another, may yet return.

The story ends with a quiet sense of hope—but also the shadow of an ever-present mystery, as Maya looks out over Echo Park, knowing her legacy will live on in the hearts of those who choose to stand against the dark forces of control.